Also by Ron Savage

NOVELS

Scar Keeper

Sharing Atmosphere

Cheap Meat

The Dreaming Field

Saving Face

Nasty Creatures

Meeting on the Steps to Hades

COLLECTIONS

Loving You the Way I Do

NOVELETTES

River of the Pink Dolphin

What We Do For Love

Tales from a Darker Heartland

Ron Savage

Fomite

Burlington, VT

ISBN-13: 978-1-942515-32-6

Library of Congress Control Number: 2015956259

Fomite

58 Peru StrBurlington, VT 05401

www.fomitepress.com

To my Janny

for the generosity of your love

A stranger has come
To share my room in the house not right in the head
A girl as mad as birds

— Dylan Thomas
"Love in the Asylum"

Some stories in this collection were originally published in the following journals: "American Illustrator" *Washington Square Review*; "Dangerous Boy" *Copper Nickel*; "Ant Life" *Portland Review*; "American Daredevil" *Crazyhorse*; Their Days Before Maine" *The Puritan*; "Dirty Martinis" *North American Review*; "The Bush Street Whores" *Louisville Review*; "The Last Time I Came Home to You" *Mochila Review*; "Little Gypsies" *The Summerset Review*; "Considering Her at Harry's Bar" *Bombay Gin*; "American Pastor" *The Baltimore Review*; Impalement Artists" *Existere*; "What Fire Does" *Main Street Rag*; "What We do for Love" *New Delta Review*; "A Beggar's Life" *Best New Writing*.

American Illustrator

ILLUSTRATOR THOMAS BLUNT died last Saturday in Venice. The brush fell from his long and steady fingers while painting an American family cheering the boat race Vogalonga on the Grand Canal. The doctor said a blood vessel had ruptured in the center of his brain. This was a good end to his life. No artist revealed American optimism better than Thomas Blunt. Critics will tell you he painted the faces we wanted to see. As if we purposely chose to ignore the darker more completed view of these faces. As if you and I conspired with the artist in an unforgivable lie. But what's wrong with such a vision? Tell me, please. What is wrong with illustrating the joyous life?

LOOK AT THOMAS Blunt's painting of the American family at the Vogalonga in Venice. There is a pink and crimson hue to the cheeks of the mother and the father, the teenage daughter and her younger brother. Frozen cheers reveal small white teeth. Sunshine has spotted the water with gold. Examine the mother leaning against the father's shoulder and see the way the light on the water is added to the blue in her eyes. Also, look at the children. Their expressions are suspended between envy and a good time. Blond curled hair edges the boy's ears.

His sister is skinny and tall and mostly legs. How often have we seen this family scene? Not enough, I say. Thomas Blunt knew how to paint Americans at play.

I am in a space between coach and business class. The airline company has named that space World Adventure Plus. I cannot stretch my legs or cross them at a reasonable angle or do one comfortable thing with any part of my middle-aged body that will give me peace. I also need to brush my teeth or at least rinse. My breath could kill a small animal.

There is a cartoon airplane on an eight inch TV attached to the seat in front of me. The cartoon plane is hovering on the edge of Greenland and the Atlantic Ocean. Everyone on the plane is flying to Washington from Heathrow. Some of us started our trip home in Venice and had travelled first to Marco Polo. I am bringing what I call "my father's body" back to Norfolk, Virginia. The coffin is stowed in the cargo area with the luggage and the tranquillized pets, but the body has more leg room than me.

What does a son do when there is nothing of a missing father but the father's work? The magazine covers, the gallery prints. Large yellowed drawing pads have been left in the attic at my mother's house, left to the shadows and the spiders. Drawing pads are stacked four and five deep and the row goes the length of the low cathedral roof. The attic has the smell of cedar and camphor. The cotton batting is wet where shingles have split and leak the rain. Mother does not protect my father's paintings and drawings.

"You're lucky I don't set the house on fire," she once told me. This was many years ago, close to thirty. Mother is a short woman and she has big ankles and a thick middle. Most of her blond hair is gray now. Her skin and hair have the scent of lavender perfume and whatever meal she is preparing: lavender perfume and tomato sauce, lavender perfume and roasted lamb. "What do you want from me?" she would say.

"You could fix the roof."

"Who exactly are you, Andrew, his lawyer?"

"I could be a lawyer." The first time I said this I was age ten and indignant beyond my years. "I'll be a lawyer and make you fix the roof," I said.

"Lawyers can earn a very nice dollar." That was usually my mother's answer. She'd say, "There's nothing wrong with a young man having a profession. " And she would kiss me on the forehead.

Forty-four years ago my father and our neighbor's fifteen year old daughter left us and went to live on the Ledo in Venice, an eight mile suburb that separates the main islands from the sea. Mother felt their departure like a hard snap of the fingers, here and gone. The daughter's name is Leah. I was seven or eight months old when this happened, and what I have is a second hand story that shifts and expands on a mood. It's a story still told with anger and bias, and I am not sure what is true and what are hurt feelings that will not heal. Thomas Blunt and fifteen year old Leah Holt have been mother's cross for years and the woman is sticking with it.

World Adventure Plus has the stink of microwaved chicken and adventurers who need a shower. It's three-seventeen in the morning. My shoes are off and my right foot is swollen and aches like knives are in my toes. I want a drug that will take the pain and my consciousness. I do not know what to do with my swollen foot. I am not a drug addict. I have never been a drug addict, and I do not want to be a drug addict at forty-four. But I am like a pregnant woman who wants the pain to go away until her child is twenty-five and has graduated college and acquired a good job.

Please give me a drug now.

I do not remember my father but mother says I am my father's son in so many ways. My hair is black and very wavy like his hair and I am tall and skinny like him. Mother swears I am a Thomas Blunt clone and has said that from day one. I have both my father's good looks and his personality, if I can believe her. Mother also praises me for keeping my promise and becoming a lawyer. My speciality is family law, child custody and support, divorce, prenuptial agreements, wills, that sort of thing. And she was right, I earn a very nice dollar.

A good son will make do, I think. That's what this good son did. A good son will study his father's illustrations and imagine the artist who painted Americans at their absolute best. A good son will imagine what would make such a man proud. Thomas Blunt's work has guided me throughout my forty-four years. His illustrations are much more than a holiday cover for a magazine or a picture for a travel brochure. My father's paintings have become a guideline on how to live my life.

One of my favorite Thomas Blunt illustrations is The Carnie (1968). In this painting we see the carnie working a three card Monte for a boy and his young father. I have imagined the carnie saying, Find the king, find the gentleman, as he uses his big hands to slide the three cards about one another on a round green felt table. Each card is creased down the middle and has the look of a miniature roof. The carnie's white shirt is rolled to the elbow and the upper sleeves are held with leather bands at the bicep. A straw flat-brimmed hat shades his eyes and most of his large nose. A cigarette hangs between thick lips and white feathered smoke is rising over the canvas tents and into the orange and yellow sunlight. Find the king, find the gentleman. When I first looked at this painting I could smell warm roasted peanuts and grilling hot dogs. Or that's what I had imagined. I could breathe in the grassy stable smell of animals. The boy is leaning over the green felt table and watching the carnie move the three cards. The boy has a narrow squint-eyed face. He is all concentration. His cheeks have a just scrubbed flush.

Find the king, find the gentleman. The young father's hand cups the boy's left shoulder. Slim fingers rest on that shoulder's bony ridge. Fingernails are curved, shaped and polished. Each cuticle is a white half moon. The father's eyes are fixed on the three cards, his mouth amused, his body close and protective. He is wearing bib overalls and a pressed navy blue t-shirt. His face and arms are tanned except for the veiny white lines that highlight the folds of his neck. He is shaved and handsome in an advertisement sort of way.

Find the king, find the gentleman.

The airplane has gone into bad weather. There is rain and we drop and rise with the air currents. Many of us in World Adventure Plus are gripping the padded armrests and staring up at the compartment where the oxygen masks are stored. The cartoon plane on the tiny TV screen in front of me is on the coastline of Nova Scotia. I am relieved to learn that my airplane does not fly directly across the Atlantic. Our pilot is intelligent and travels near land. If we crash we can easily swim to shore.

My father's wishes are not Leah's wishes. Thomas Blunt did not want his body flown back to Virginia. There was a paradox to my father. He left his country to live in Venice three days after he turned twenty-six. I was a baby when he left me and my mother. Venice had been his home for most of his life, or close to forty-four years of it. The man who had painted American optimism better than any other artist could not live in America. I think that's funny. Not ha-ha funny, I do not mean that, but interestingly funny, maybe depressingly funny.

Thomas Blunt would have gone to jail if he had stayed in America. That is what mother believed, what she used to tell me. And there was a truth to that, certainly in his younger days. "They put men in jail for what he did," Mother would say. "They put men in jail and throw away the key, Andrew. Don't you forget it." As a son, as a boy and as a man, I have tried to imagine what it is like to never come home.

My father had wanted his body buried on the island of San Michele. The tan brick wall and the tops of the cedar trees can be seen by the vapporetti on the Laguna Veneta. Ezra Pound is buried there in the permanent section and so is Igor Stravinsky. The permanent section is the place where the elite meet to rot, the immortals. Thomas Blunt was close to the permanents yet not close enough. The non-permanents on San Michelle are dug up in twenty years and carted to the mainland or placed into an ossuary, a mausoleum for bones. More than one body has been tossed into the lagoon. I'm sure a caretaker in the future will see the graves of Ezra and Igor and ask himself, Who are these two? And why have they stayed so long? He will say, There are too many for this. Bodies arrive every day. They're waiting on their turns. The caretaker will then toss Ezra and Igor into the lagoon, too.

There are no immortal bones, he will say.

I think Thomas Blunt would have liked the way I am living my life. I have studied his paintings, his visions of family and country, how he expressed the American grasp of right and wrong. If my father could paint a life, the life painted would be mine. I am the good son, and I was the good student. My friends are many and they are loyal and caring and I am humbled by their kindness and their devotion. The importance of friendship is in all my father's paintings. Another theme throughout Thomas Blunt's work is America's faith in our lord and savior. I have also learned that from him. I met my wife, Jessie Lynn Combs, when mother and I began attending church. I was nine then and Jessie Lynn was a year younger and we loved each other from the start. Jess and I have been married for twenty-five years and we are blessed with three children who have never caused us a regret. Who among of us, especially in today's world, can say that? Not many, I bet.

My left foot has gone from swollen and feeling like knives are in my toes to swollen and numb. Three times I have hobbled down the aisle of World Adventure Plus to stir my middle aged circulation. When I reach the blue and gray curtain separating World Adventure Plus from coach class, I have peeked into that section to reassure myself that things could be worse. The people in coach have nothing behind their eyes and smell of dirty socks. They are like the living dead. They drink warm water out of foggy plastic bottles. I am sure their souls left their bodies somewhere over the North Atlantic.

Many of us are sleeping now. But a few adventurers watch movies on the small monitors. The movies are the ones we did not want to watch in the theaters. Dim screens are filled with bad acting and no plots and jokes that go no where. The plane is dark and I can hear everyone's private sounds. These are the sounds people make when they are alone or with people who know them and love them.

The cartoon plane on the monitor attached to the back of the seat in front of me is flying over Bar Harbor and the tiny plane looks as unruffled and determined as the hour it lifted off from London.

"You are his son, Andrew."

"What am I supposed to do?"

This was the phone conversation I'd had with Leah, the talk that brought me to Venice. I knew what my father saw in her the first time I met her there. Leah is fifty-seven years old and still a beauty. Her arms and legs are long, slim and tan, and there is hardly a line on her face. Oh maybe a few lines at the corners of her eyes but not many, believe me. Her hair is mostly white with a streak or two of black and she wears her hair in a loose ponytail. She is startlingly lovely, one of those natural beauties with turquoise eyes and a chin and cheekbones you would kill for.

But on this day and this phone call she was a face I did not know and a voice I had never heard.

"Is that really what you want for him?" Leah said. The voice was composed and direct. It side stepped volume but did not do away with its warmth. "You want him to stay here? Stay in this foreign place, so far from his people? Do you know what an ossuary is, Andrew? It's a box for bones. Are you listening? He'll get that if he is lucky. If he's lucky. I know the diggers at San Michele. Bodies are thrown into the lagoon all the time. No son would want that for a father."

"How are you getting along?"

"How do you think?" She said this a little snappy, I thought.

"If you prefer not to get into things, that's okay."

"I've been in a panic, Andrew. An absolute panic. I don't want the diggers to hurt him. I don't want them to throw away his body."

I am talking to her, I had thought. But I could not hold onto that idea. I could not feel it for more than a second or two without stepping away. My father is dead and I am talking to her. That's what I had thought. And I listened to Leah and heard my mother's angry stories, every obsession, every wound. These are stories children take on as their own. We hold these stories close to keep what is left of our families. Leah Holt was the girl, the adolescent, Thomas Blunt had loved better than his wife and his son. Father and Leah had lived in Venice for almost as many years as I have been on the planet.

"I want him buried in America," Leah said.

"Is that what he wanted?"

"He was an American artist, Andrew. That's what he painted."

"I want what he wanted," I said.

And I had my own idea about what Thomas Blunt wanted. Home is where you live your life. He had loved Leah enough to start a new home with her in Venice. He missed America and painted what he missed but he loved Leah and he lived in Venice.

Father wanted his body buried on the island of San Michele. He knew he was not Ezra Pound or Igor Stravinsky and would never be one of the permanents. That did not matter. My father would take his chances at San Michele, take the twenty years, take the ossuary, take the bottom of the Laguna Veneta. He would consider it an honor. Thomas Blunt loved America but he loved his Leah more and he painted the rest.

I wonder how the body is doing in the cargo hull with the luggage and the tranquilized pets. I cannot rid myself of the envy and imagine swapping the coffin for my seat. Why do the dead have coffins when the living need the leg room?

The cartoon airplane on the small screen attached to the seat in front of me is over Casco Bay and heading toward Kennebunkport. World Adventure Plus now smells of bad vegetables. Another thing, I do not have any feeling from the waist down. That is not completely true. My left hip is burning at the joint but the trip is almost done and the pain will not stop that. I can go through anything to get my feet on airport concrete.

Once again Thomas Blunt's work has helped me solve the dilemma of how to please the artist and the woman who loved him. The diggers at San Michele are not above accepting a euro or two. Even in mid-February the island is beautiful. It has tan brick walls and tall cedars and white marble tombstones and mausoleums. The sky is mostly gray and clouded in the winter and there is a cold sharp wind that ruffles the lagoon and blows the dust between the stones. I can smell the sea and the bones. Or I think I can. San Michelle has bodies waiting and bodies in the ground. Bodies are everywhere, more than you know. And I walk among the rows of new coffins and think of Thomas Blunt's painting The Carnie. I think of the man with the straw brimmed hat that shaded his eyes and much of his nose. A cigarette hangs between his thick lips and the white feathered smoke drifts over the canvas tents and into an orange and yellow sun. Find the king, find the gentleman, he says. The boy is leaning over the green felt table and watching the carnie move the three creased cards with his big graceful hands. The boy has a squinty-eyed face. He is all concentration. His cheeks have a just scrubbed flush. Find the king, find the gentleman, the carnie says. I can smell roasted peanuts and grilling hot dogs. I breathe in the grassy stable smell of the animals. A young father's hand has cupped the boy's left shoulder. The father's eyes are fixed on the three cards, his mouth amused, his body close and protective.

Impalement Artists

He is passing them in the lobby of the movie theater and smiles at Nelson's new wife the way a man does when he has a secret about the wife that the husband doesn't know. Mr. Happy, Nelson thinks to himself. Mr. Happy has the smug beefy look of a wrestler. He is short but with thick arms and legs. Nelson and Butler have been waiting at the concession stand.

"Who was that?" Nelson says.

His new wife is looking at the candy and the popcorn.

"I don't have a clue," she says.

Nelson has a new job as an orderly in an Alzheimer's facility and he is now thinking about a resident there named Edelina who believes he is her dead husband. Nelson has talked to her enough to know how her mind works.

"I hated the carnivals," Edelina says. "What sort of job was that? Why did you put me into those situations?"

The top half of her hospital bed is raised to a sitting position. She has white hair clipped above the ear like a man's haircut with bristled sides and a top combed straight back. Edelina is small and bony, her hands, her fingers, her pretty face. There are crisscrossed lines about the eyes and lines at the corners of her mouth. Her skin is like worn silk. The room smells of urine and disinfectant and Nelson must breathe through his mouth to avoid the stink.

"Your knives always missed me unless you were angry," Edelina says. "That's when the knives cut. I have scars on my shoulders and the inside of my legs. I have too many scars from you."

Nelson and his new bride are on the green and umber sofa in their living room watching cable news. They were married June 2nd, last month. Butler is six months pregnant. Her blond hair has been pulled back into a ponytail and secured with a thick beige rubber band. She smells of orange scented bath soap. Her sleeveless nightie ends at mid-thigh. Butler's arms and legs are long and thin and too white. Each day Nelson watches her belly become larger. This can't be my life, he thinks. Nelson does not like Butler, let alone love her. Everything about his wife irritates him. Butler breathes through her mouth when she sleeps and makes a gargled choking sound. She has restless leg syndrome and will kick him at night without warning. Nelson does not like her adjusting his shirt collar and fooling with the front of his hair before he goes to school or his job at the hospital. Butler will not close her mouth when she chews her food. And another thing. She watches forensics on TV and says, "Oh that's creepy, oh that's creepy," every five minutes.

Lately Butler has been telling him what to do with his life.

"Nobody needs a Ph.D., Nelson," she says. "Daddy's absolutely right, you should stop feeling superior to everybody and get yourself a job like a grown up." Butler also likes to say, "For a smart person, Nelson, you really are low rent."

Nelson thinks this is what goes on when people do the wrong thing followed by the right thing.

Light from the TV spreads into the dark living room like a big luminous fan. Butler is holding Nelson's hand on her lap and his fingers are numb. He has on a white t-shirt and navy blue Rayon boxers that show different types of gold dogs in profile. Nelson is skinny like Butler but his hair is black and curled and hides the rims of his ears. His arms and legs are hairy. Butler likes using her fingernails to comb his arms.

Nelson's best friend says Nelson should thank God he married Butler. The best friend can't believe Nelson's luck.

"What a hot bitch," Wayne tells him.

Butler is the department's secretary and twenty years old, three years younger than Nelson. Wayne and Nelson are both doctoral students in the neuropsych program at Virginia Commonwealth University. Wayne has an overbite and bad skin and likes playing online games with his laptop. He is a level forty-eight battlemage who is in love with a dark elf.

Butler and Nelson had their first talk by the vestibule closet during last year's Christmas social at Professor Grishbaum's home in downtown Richmond. That night the snow cut power lines from Charlottesville to Franklin. Wind slanted and trembled the snow. Snow blew across the Moonlight. Snow hid the sidewalks and the mailboxes and the cars parked along the street. Grishbaum had lighted cedar logs in a blackened stone fireplace. Flames from the cedar brought hard shadows to the creases of Grishbaum's face and beneath his thick eyebrows. Students were talking and lighting candles and drinking. Mostly Gin and grapefruit juice, Nelson remembered. Candlelight showed on the walls and the ceiling. Butler and Nelson had ended their night inside the vestibule closet with the smell of leather and wet wool. Butler was biting her fist, one thin leg hooked around Nelson.

"People get married and have children," this is what Butler's mother always said. Her father would say, "That's what separates us from the animals."

Butler's parents are slim and clean looking and smelled of talcum. The father has black hair parted in the middle and the mother has blond hair like Butler. Sometimes her parents wear matching pastel sweaters.

Butler once told Nelson what her parents had told her.

"People get married and have children," she'd said. "That's what separates us from the animals."

Nelson stared down at the cracked gray pavement.

"Whooping Cranes mate for life," he had said.

Three weeks after the night in the Grishbaum vestibule closet Butler called her boyfriend, Georgie, and told him what he needed to do.

"Listen, it's me and I'm pregnant," she said. "It's not your baby but you're the person I love. All right, okay? My baby should have a father and I want you to marry me."

Georgie said, "Hello? Hello? Who is this?"

"You know who this is, you low rent moron."

Then Georgie said, "Wait. You're calling to abuse me? This is how you do business? Nothing about how sorry you are for betraying my trust? Nothing about, 'Will you ever forgive me?' Nothing like that?" Georgie doesn't wait for her answer. "Hey I tell you what," he said. "Call the kid's real father and abuse him."

The nurse is explaining a quirk of Alzheimer's to Nelson.

"You can see out the window and you know the person on the other side of that window." she says. The nurse has big pink legs and dyed blond hair wrapped in a French twist. Colors and lines from a tattoo on the calf of one big leg are faded to an unrecognizable shape. Nelson knows about Alzheimer's but has been told by his advisor not to interrupt the hospital staff. "Here's the deal," the nurse says. "Your window may last five minutes or maybe longer but the window will go away."

After the nurse leaves the room Nelson smiles at his patient.

"Where were we, Miss E.?"

Nelson is sitting beside Edelina's bed. He has been reading to her. What Nelson reads are clippings from a scrapbook. The names Zando The Magnificent and The Exotic Edelina are printed in boxy gold letters across the leather cover. One clipping is on Edelina and her husband touring the world for twenty-six years. The article calls Zando a great impalement artist. Nelson doesn't know if the old woman is hearing what he reads to her. He isn't sure if she even knows he is in the room. But five days a week Nelson combs her hair and feeds her dinner and reads the scrapbook to her.

She is lying flat on the bed watching the shadowed ceiling. The room has mint green walls and a polished gray tile floor. Two ceiling fans rotate their blades and cool nothing. An odor of urine and pine oil clots the air.

"Don't be threatening me with your knives, Zando," the old woman says while watching the ceiling.

Today someone else, a nurse's aide, combed Edelina's hair. It's all spiked on top like a punk rocker. Nelson brushes her white hair straight back until the spikes are gone.

"There you go, Miss E.," he says. "That's definitely more you."

She is in the carnival again with her husband, Nelson thinks. He steps to the edge of Edelina's bed and holds her hand. The hand feels like sticks and paper. Her white nightgown is loose enough about her neck to reveal a bony shoulder.

"I have too many scars," Edelina says.

"I'm not Zando," Nelson tells her. He wears his red and white striped golf shirt and he is scratching the hair on his arm with his fingernails. Tiny white flecks spot the forearm under the hair. Then Nelson says, "Forget the knives and the carnivals. Don't you worry about those days, Miss E. Okay? Look at me, please. You know your husband and you know my face isn't his face."

There are fewer lines at the corners of Edelina's eyes now.

Fewer lines along her forehead, too. Her skin is more flushed than yesterday. She has lost ten years the way some people on a diet can lose a fast ten pounds. Nelson sees this when the old woman turns her head to him. It's the afternoon light from the window. It's the angle of her face.

Edelina touches the tiny white flecks on his bare arm with her fingertips. "Poor thing," she says.

Nelson has his own scars. His mother liked wearing silver rings and turquoise and silver bracelets. When she hit him, the rings and the bracelets would leave cuts on his arms and the back of his neck and on his lower legs. Oh, Miss E., the stories we could swap, Nelson thinks this and almost says it but doesn't. His mother was a beauty, her dark hair draped on narrow freckled shoulders, her eyes big enough to swallow you. She was beautiful and too young for babies and wanted to enjoy her life. What do you do when you want to enjoy your life but your baby won't shut up? His mother used to say his father was an old friend who lived in another town and one day they would visit him.

"Be good and you and me will go visit daddy," she used to say, but they never did.

Nelson liked telling his mother about the things he learned in school. He liked showing his drawings to her and reading his book reports out loud and explaining how the sun and the moon and the earth made an eclipse.

"You don't know it all," she'd say. There was a hurt sound to her voice. "You need to get off that high horse, sonny boy."

Somewhere in the day his mother would stop feeling hurt and start feeling angry.

The sunlight in Edelina's hospital room glistens the tile floor and the far mint green wall. Nelson is hiding his forearm with the flat of his right hand so Edelina cannot see the scars. He doesn't feel comfortable talking about his scars or his mother, not yet. Last night Nelson woke up next to Butler and looked at his arms and thought the scars were tiny white worms trying to break loose from under his skin.

Butler and Nelson are still sitting on the green and umber sofa in the living room. Light from the TV splits the dark room into silver and shadow. Butler is wearing her sleeveless teddy that ends at mid-thigh. Her thin pale legs are crossed at the knee. She holds Nelson's hand while they look at the war on cable news. Nelson is saying the president should take medication. That's when Butler's cell starts vibrating against the glass coffee table.

Before she can say yeah who is this she hears Georgie tell her, "You looked too great at the movies. Just too great. I'm going to do it. We'll get married. I've thought about your kid and all and I love you and we'll get married like you want. I have one very reasonable condition."

"You have the wrong number," she says.

"You can't call me and tell me you're pregnant and expect me to go, 'Oh okay,' just like that. A person has to think about the situation. This is very serious shit. Okay? I need to consider your verbal abuse. Do I want to marry an abuser? That's the question I asked myself. So I figure we'll try marriage counseling."

Butler sighs and looks at the dark ceiling and says, "No one lives here by that name." She clicks off her cell phone.

"Who was that?" Nelson wants to know.

"I don't have a clue," she says.

The next day at work Nelson is listening to Edelina talk about her dead husband. "Zando would say, 'You think you're better than me.' I'd get that all the time."

The top half of Edelina's bed is again locked in an upright position. For the past five minutes her thinking has been clear. The nurse with the big legs and the tattoo has described this as Edelina's momentary reprieve from Alzheimer's. Sunlight reflects off the gray tile floor. The smell of cut grass comes through the open window along with the sound of a gas mower. Nelson is rubbing moisturizer over Edelina's bony arms. Her skin feels papery but Nelson thinks she looks younger than she did yesterday. Fewer crisscross lines are at the corners of her eyes. Or perhaps she does not look younger, Nelson isn't sure, but she does look more alive when she can see him and talk to him.

"I wasn't better than my husband," Edelina says. "I was smarter. Zando left school in the eighth grade. He never cracked a book. What did he know? I had two years of college before my father used the money for other things. I was a reader. My husband never forgave me."

Nelson tells Edelina about his mother and can hear the quiver in his voice. Then he tells her about his marriage and the baby. Nelson squeezes more lotion from a plastic bottle into the palm of his hand. The lotion smells of lavender. He rubs the lotion onto Edelina's small bony arm, her paper skin.

"I married a woman who is too familiar," Nelson says. "When I am around her I get upset with how she is and things that have nothing to do with her. I don't know what is right but I wanted to do right. For both her and the baby," he says. "I don't want my kid feeling alone the way I felt alone."

Edelina is looking at the two ceiling fans. The dark blades rotate through the afternoon sunlight. The shadows of the blades move above her.

She has started talking to herself. "Your knives always missed me unless you were angry," she says. "That's when the knives cut."

Nelson rubs the lavender scented lotion on her elbows and hands. He works the lotion into her fingers.

"I can respect people," Edelina says. "I am a respectful person. I see the good in people." Edelina is with her dead husband and Nelson doesn't know what to do, how to get her out. "You were never the husband for me," she says and watches the fan blades move the shadows on the ceiling. "I was too scared to tell you," she says. "No, that's not true. I'll tell you what's true. I was too scared to find another life."

There is a car parked in Nelson's assigned space at the apartment complex. It's close to 10:00 PM and people are home and most of the parking spaces are filled. Nelson parks near the corner. The parking lot smells of gasoline and the garbage from the green metal dumpsters and whatever had been cooked for supper. Moonlight and the lamps from the apartments show on the cars, vans and pickups.

A young man is now leaving Nelson's apartment building. He goes to his car in Nelson's assigned space and unlocks the door on the driver's side. It's the guy who smiled at Butler in the movie theater.

"Mr. Happy," Nelson says to himself.

Mr. Happy is fifteen pounds beefier than Nelson remembered. He is short but with big thick arms and legs. Nelson first thinks he will grab Mr. Happy by his thick neck and tell him to keep his car out of his parking space. He will tell him to find a woman who isn't married. Nelson thinks this as Mr. Happy is driving out of the parking lot.

"What do you mean what am I doing?" Butler says.

"You know what I mean," Nelson says.

Butler is getting all huffy and holier-than-thou which is what Butler does when she has done something she doesn't want to discuss. Nelson knows his wife. Butler and Nelson are in their living room with its green and umber sofa and glass kidney shaped coffee table and a wall to wall carpet that lost its color years ago. Butler has an unlighted cigarette wedged between two stiff manicured fingers. Her cheeks and forehead are flushed and she keeps brushing a long strand of blond hair away from her eyes. The apartment smells of cigarettes.

"Since when do you smoke?"

"Since none of your business," Butler says.

Nelson goes to work the following morning. There is no

one in Edelina's room and the bare gray mattress lays on the box spring. Nelson touches the mattress with his palm. The nurse with the big legs and the tattoo tells him that Edelina died in the night. Dusty sunshine hovers above the tile floor. The light changes the color of the mint green wall opposite the window to gold. The room still has the smell of urine and pine oil. A plastic bottle of lotion is on the nightstand next to the bed. The nurse said Edelina had outlived all her relatives and her friends. Edelina's leather scrapbook has been left for Nelson at the foot of the box spring. Inside the scrapbook are photographs of a beautiful young Edelina wearing a black sequined body suit. She is small and delicate with short dark hair. She poses in profile against a velvet background, her back arched, a thin arm raised. There are also photos of Zando holding two silver knives in each hand. He has on a black body suit like Edelina's but with narrow stripes down his legs and arms. Zando used a blindfold when he threw his knives. Edelina would tap the board next to her and Zando would throw a knife toward the sound. The photos look as old and fragile as the old woman. Each photo is dated on the back in ink, Brazil 1923, England 1931, New York 1925, Paris 1929, hundreds of photographs in no particular order.

There is a new feeling in Nelson that he cannot name. He imagines the old woman sitting up on the bed, her small bones and her paper skin. His stomach has started to cramp. Nelson is breathing through his mouth to avoid the stink of urine and the pine oil but his eyes are burning and the back of his throat feels swollen. The old woman Nelson imagines on the bed has refused to stay put and he is again confronted with the box spring and the bare gray mattress. Nelson presses his left arm to his chest and begins rubbing the tiny white flecks beneath the dark hair.

He can hear the jangle of silver and turquoise bracelets.

"You need to get off that high horse, sonny boy." His mother's words have a wounded sound.

Nelson does not tell the nurse with the big legs and the tattoo that he is leaving but after finishing half his shift that's what he does. He drives out of the parking lot and into downtown Richmond traffic. The evening is warm and damp and the sky between and above the buildings has become an orange and maroon.

Exhaust fumes and the smell of fast food burgers enter the car through the open window on the driver's side. A few cars have turned on their headlights and the lights pass Nelson like quick intrusions.

He has decided to leave Butler. He will wait a year or two or perhaps three but he will do it.

Leaving someone requires a very good plan, Nelson thinks. He imagines a Sunday afternoon.

"Daddy, let's get an ice cream," his boy or girl says.

"I don't see why not." Nelson kneels eye-level to the child. "Tell mommy we are going for an ice cream while I start the car."

Nelson's mother used to tell him that his father was an old

friend who lived in another town and one day they would visit but they never did. Nelson might drive to Williamsburg or Norfolk for an ice cream. He will have extra napkins in the glove compartment to wipe his child's sticky hands and face. Kids love to make a mess. After ice cream they could keep driving, Virginia Beach, Charlotte, Chapel Hill, maybe stop and visit his mother's old friend. Nelson would not mind.

Dirty Martinis

My wife had gone on a weekend trip to Norfolk for a hospital administrators conference and took our little girl to my mother's. All that was years ago now. I told Eve I would patch the roof and do some gutter work I had been putting off.

"Do what you want, Leon," she'd said. But later in the afternoon I quit the roof work and filled up the Chevy Nova and drove to our cabin twenty or so miles from Front Royal in the Blue Ridge. The air smelled of bailed hay and pine and it was cold enough to see my breath. Sunlight glared on the waxed hood of the Chevy. Even with my sunglasses the road was not easy to see. Maples and oaks were colored red and orange and lime and many leaves had pasted themselves onto the road. Clouds along the mountains tops threaded the horizon.

On that late afternoon I saw Eve's Toyota parked in front of our small one window cabin. A rusted yellow 150 Ford pick up was there beside the Toyota. I knew who owned that one, too.

THE SECRET TO a good Dirty Martini is olive brine but not much of it. Brine will give the martini an opaque color and a salty and ever so slight bittersweet taste and works fine with very cold vodka. I am telling my daughter this and I also tell her how she must begin a Dirty Martini by rubbing vermouth inside the glass. Rickie has been listening to me and nodding and saying breathy uh-huhs while rotating a strand of her hair around a slim forefinger. She is seated on the opposite side of the blond wood butcher's block in the kitchen. I see some of myself in her, the dark eyes and hair, the skin so easily tanned. Some of her mother is there too, that small sculpted nose, those cheekbones.

"My martinis never taste right," Rickie says. She has a conquered look. Her perfume is a citrus fragrance, lemons, I think. Makeup covers a green and purple bruise at the right edge of her eye but the makeup does not do a decent job. That side of her face is puffy from her eye to her jaw. "My martinis never taste like your's," she says. "I absolutely love your martinis. But mine, I don't know. I end up pouring every stupid thing I fix into the sink. Your daughter has jars and jars of olives with no brine," she says. Rickie will talk about herself in the third person.

I HAD PARKED my Chevy Nova beneath the clustered shadow of three large oaks, maybe thirty yards from the cabin. My hands were still holding the steering wheel and I could hear my breath and the hard rhythm of my heart. Eve was at the window but she was not looking at any particular thing and her face had no expression. She wore a flowered red and lavender robe that must have been new. I could not remember seeing her in it. Gray smoke was drifting up from the brick chimney. Smoke unraveled in the cold air. I tried picturing our bedroom closet and the robe hanging there with her other clothes but the images did not go together. The robe was sheer and showed my wife's thin silhouette, her protruding belly, her breasts thick and weary and lovely. I knew every blemish and childhood scar on her body, that's what I was thinking. Then Eve disappeared from the small window and the window was dark and empty. My wife's other life. Mysterious, dissatisfied Eve. We are married and I am part of her but she is not with me now, I was thinking that, too.

I looked at the yellow pick up parked next to my wife's Toyota by the front steps of our cabin. There was a Virginia Tech decal on the rusted silver bumper and a "Carter-Mondale '80" sticker next to that. The Ford 150 belonged to my brother. Thomas was two years younger than me but married just as long and had twin baby girls. He taught Western Civ at Blue Ridge Community College. His features were delicate and pretty like our mother, angular cheekbones and long fingers. There was an easy way about him and he could tell a joke better than anybody I knew. Thomas and Eve had always liked one another.

SUNLIGHT IS SLANTING across the blond wood butcher's block from the three skylights over counter. Dusty gold particles float between my daughter and me. My far too skinny daughter, I think. Lacquered walls and kitchen appliances are white and reflect the afternoon sun. Copper pans hang on a metal rack above us.

Eve and I divorced when our Rickie was seven. I still work as a psychologist in the same hospital outside of Richmond where Eve and I first met. I work with people who see things and hear things that are not there and not true. And the families are just as crazy as the relatives they put into the hospital. Show me a crazy person and I'll show you a crazy family. Twenty-eight years have passed and I cannot forgive my ex-wife. After we divorced Eve became born again, an evangelical, and she left her hospital administrator job. Now my ex-wife brings Jesus to third world countries.

"Would you have recognized your daughter?" Rickie wants to know.

She has not left third person mode. Rickie leans toward her raised martini glass and her sip is fast and audible.

"Not in a million years," I say and that's the unfortunate truth.

I have not seen my daughter since she was a baby. This is our second get together in a month. Rickie wore large sunglasses the first time and her visit lasted less than an hour. She had left the house without a good-bye or closing the front door. We were both very nervous, I guess.

Rickie is not wearing sunglasses on this visit. The green and purple bruise at the corner of her eye is new.

"My therapist thinks these visits are key," my daughter says. She has on thready jeans and her white t-shirt shows beneath a forest green leather jacket. Rickie is watching her fingers grip the stem of the martini glass. Her nails have been filed to the skin and painted red. This is the M.O. of a nail biter, a contemplator of anxious thoughts. Her citrus perfume hovers about the butcher's block with the sunlight. "My therapist really likes the whole checking out reality thing," she says.

Rickie is thirty-five or very close to it. Her free hand rakes through the back of her curled dark hair. The bruised side of her face has a swollen temple and jaw and I wonder if she knows enough to take an aspirin or an ibuprofen.

Rickie left school and home in the tenth grade and hitch-hiked to Colorado with a bag of apples and thirty-five dollars. My daughter thought she wanted to marry some guy thirty years older than her. The guy built and painted cars and shaved his eyebrows. He looked like that film actor who played Dracula. This was the story I got on her first visit. I do not know what she knows and what she does not know.

I have pictured God talking to me. "Leon, God says, "Look, I realize Eve humped your brother who you loved and trusted. Tommy is an asshole son of a bitch if there ever was one. I also know preparing people for these heartbreaks is not the best thing I do. So I am atoning for that by bringing your lovely young daughter back into your life."

This is how most Jews think God does His work. The Jews suspect God is fallible but will admit His errors and rectify them. Jews argue with God. Christians do not get this. The Muslims and the Christians pray and hope God will answer. Jews want God to consider other avenues He may have missed.

"I'm happy you're here," I say to Rickie. And that is the truth.

"Your daughter is happy too, daddy," she says.

SHADOWS BLACKENED THE hood of the Chevy Nova. I had not moved from under the three large oaks. I was twenty-five or thirty yards from our cabin and just to the left. My car smelled like an old party. Eve's cork tipped cigarette butts filled the ash tray and some of the cork tips were stained with dry cherry red lipstick. Empty cardboard pizza boxes and balled up wrappers from cheeseburgers cluttered the backseat and the black plastic mats on the floor. Psychologists will tell you that many orderly people have one sloppy area. One secret messy place. It might be a closet or the corner of a basement or a bathroom that nobody uses but you. My sloppy area was my Chevy Nova.

"Why don't you ever clean out the backseat or empty your ashtray?" Eve would ask me. I had no answer and still don't have one. I also ignore feelings I do not want the way I ignore the empty pizza boxes in the backseat. I will ignore feelings that do not match the person I think I am. We love to fool ourselves.

I had lost my wife and that simple place we enjoyed together. That was what I thought sitting there in the Chevy Nova. I watched the stringy smoke curl and flutter out the brown brick chimney. I pictured the sparks and orange ash in the stone and mortar fireplace. We bought our one window cabin the first year we were married. We bought the cabin from a man my wife and I called the Mad Bomber. He had chestnut and gray hair that he never combed and his eyes were blue and nervous. Eve and I liked to joke about finding his explosives tucked away in a wall or a floorboard. We spent our first two weekends scrubbing the soot from the window and the sulfur and the damp earth smell from every surface we could find.

Maybe I am stalling with these thoughts. I am hoping every hurtful thing will go away. Good-bye to my wife's Toyota and my brother's yellow 150 Ford pick up. Good-bye to my wife's flowered red and lavender bathrobe that I had not seen in our closet. Good-bye and good luck to all concerned. I felt paralyzed. I did not know how to instruct my hand to open a car door. Who would want to climb our cabin steps and go into such a situation? If I did climb those steps and knock on that door, what would come next? Do we sit down and discuss our situation like the Brits having tea and biscuits in a sunny room? Should we approach it the old fashioned American way and beat the shit out of each other?

Or was it time for a pistol or a knife and what gangsters call "permanent solutions." I could not imagine anyone rushing into our one window cabin but the local TV news.

A WHITE SLASH of sun crosses the butcher's block. Rickie is

sipping her martini and the sunlight has turned the right half of her face into an overexposed photograph.

"Your daughter never had any luck with males," Rickie says. "I go for the hulking, concrete types. Guys strong enough to protect me but disinterested enough not to get involved. Navy Seals and your police detectives, those types. Then she says, "Men and martinis."

Rickie does not look at me when she says this but she smiles to herself and has another audible sip of her martini. For a second or two my daughter's thin shoulders go up and down as if she is keeping the rhythm to a song I cannot hear. The parts of her face outside the sunlight include the green and purple bruise at the corner of her eye.

"My therapist says my life is a bad fairy tale," Rickie says. "Can you imagine? I pay somebody to tell me shit like that."

I take the first sip of my own martini. It's been sitting on the butcher's block in the sun for twenty minutes or more and the glass is warm and the vodka has lost its chill. I ask Rickie if anyone is protecting her from the men who protect her. I know I am showing off. That's the bad news and good news of being a psychologist for thirty-some years. I have heard way too many scenarios.

"Not even Jesus," she says and her shoulders do not miss a beat.

Behind Rickie are double glass doors that open onto a gray wood deck that has a tinted glass table, an umbrella, and four wrought iron chairs with gray and navy blue cushions. The cushions match the umbrella. My daughter is looking over her shoulder at the glass doors. This is the third time I have seen her do that. She must be plotting a getaway.

"I used to imagine you were like a Navy Seal or a police detective," Rickie says. Her voice is too quiet and I ask her to repeat what she just said and my daughter says the sentence again but she says it while looking at the sunlight on the blond wood butcher's block and not at me. "I used to imagine you punching out anybody who gave you shit," my daughter says. Her citrus perfume mixes with the sunny and dusty light. "Mother would go nuts if she knew I was here," Rickie tells me. "Mother thinks you are the devil."

"What do you think?" I say.

"Your daughter doesn't know you," she says.

I had left the Chevy Nova parked under the three oaks. Eve stood at the window in that flowered red and lavender bathrobe. I watched her as I walked down the path toward the cabin steps. Rust, orange and lime leaves were scattered on the path and the late afternoon sunlight pressed through the oaks and pines in long white angles. The mountains smelled of damp wood and grass and the air was cold and stung my cheeks and forehead. Eve stood by the window and looked at me like I was an automobile accident or some mangled creature on the side of the road. Smoke caught the breeze and twisted and scattered from the brick chimney. When I think back to that late afternoon I think Eve must have been very frightened but at that time, walking toward the cabin, walking into a situation, I did not know anything or feel anything. And I had no idea what I was going to do. It was one step at a time, one foot in front of the other.

I knocked on the door and waited for Eve or Thomas to answer but nobody did and I used the flat of my foot to splinter the door from its hinge. The force of my foot against the door and the door breaking from the wood frame startled me. I did not know I had such a choice and I did not know I had decided on that choice. My strength and what it felt like to use my strength was all new to me.

My wife screamed. She was standing in a far dark corner with one thin arm crossing the front of her flowered red and lavender robe while her other arm was raised above her head. Eve screamed again and the hand above her head started quivering and batting at the air. Our cabin smelled of fried meat and my wife's cigarettes. There was also a cooked broccoli smell. White sunshine cut through the window shadows and made a narrow and brilliant line over the floor and the wood table in the center of the room. Our silver and black china dishes were on the table. Eve and I bought the china for our cabin. I remembered our meals here and our conversations during this or that meal. Food lay on the plates, a half eaten hamburger and bun, a plastic mint green tray of sliced tomatoes and Bermuda onions, a relish jar, mustard and ketchup bottles, a glass of soda not finished. I cleared the table with a single sweep of my arm. China, condiments and food flew everywhere. The ketchup bottle landed on the hot orange ash in the fireplace. The bottle melted and turned black. My wife screamed for the third time and I heard myself growl at her.

Brother Tommy sat on edge of the unmade bed at the opposite corner from Eve. He was wearing white jockeys and shadows hid his right side. The part of him in the sunlight was thin, bleached and delicate. His chest had no hair and his ribs and his veins were visible. As Tommy started to get up from the bed I hit him across the face. I hurt my hand when I hit him but I hit him two more times, a second time in the face and one hard punch to the upper arm. Tommy and I were not fighters. We never fought with each other or anyone else, even in high school. We were the sons a mother could love. At the end of the fight my hand was bruised and fractured. Tommy had a cracked left cheekbone that would leave his pretty face less than perfect.

Eve screamed at me throughout the fight.

"Who are you, Leon?" she kept saying. "You're a stranger. What sort of man does this?"

I felt heat on my shoulders and my neck from the stone fireplace. Many people expect your profession to make you into somebody besides yourself.

"YOU DIDN'T WANT to see your daughter?" Rickie says this while looking down at what is left of her second martini. Her words are a soft and hungry sound. The afternoon sunlight goes across the blond butcher's block between us. Rickie's hands look colorless in the brilliant light, little hands with fingernails filed to the skin and painted red. The fingertips have a tremor. Her citrus perfume is strong in the kitchen. "I was angry at everybody," Rickie says. "Mother used to tell me you were the devil but refused to tell me why. I pictured you as this big shot guy who didn't care about anybody."

"The big shot part is wrong," I say and take a slow sip of the martini.

The tension has been leaving my stomach and chest for the past fifteen minutes. Thank God for the dirty martini. My daughter is on the other side of the afternoon sun. It's coming through the three skylights above the Formica counter. The light splitting the blond wood butcher's block has turned dusty yellow. What I do not say to Rickie is this, for a while I did not care about her or anyone. A disturbing truth but my own. What can a person do? When I did allow myself to care again, too much time had come and gone.

"Guys are bullies," she is saying. Her finger and thumb twist a dark curl of hair. She has her mother's cheekbones, her sculpted nose. Eve is always present in my daughter. I cannot ignore that. "Every guy I date a has rotten attitude," Rickie says but she will not look at me. You can hear the anger in her. Then she says, "You name the rotten attitude and I've dated it. And God help anyone who tells Mr. Wonderful to get an attitude adjustment. Guys do not want to hear that shit." Rickie's index and middle fingers trace the side of her bruised and swollen face. "Guess why I got this?" she says.

"Does that happen a lot?" I want to know.

"What's a lot?" she says.

My daughter has turned her head to look beyond the kitchen and the double glass doors that lead to the deck. She is checking out the woods behind my house. Remembering her escape route, perhaps. I reach for Rickie's hand through the sunshine but the hand withdraws from my touch. Her martini glass tips and shatters on the polished oak floor. Right away my daughter is on her hands and knees gathering the shards of the martini glass.

"Wait, wait," I say and start to help her.

"It's an accident," she tells me. "People have accidents," she says. Her voice is breathy and very close to panic. "You can't expect a person not to have an accident," she says.

I sit back on the bar stool and watch. Shards of the martini glass flash in the afternoon sunlight. Her arms and hands move here and there. Fingers capture the broken glass and drop them into a cupped hand. My daughter is talking to herself. "Jesus, Jesus," she is saying. "Jesus, Jesus." Rickie has cut herself but she does not quit. Her fingers and her cupped palm are bloody.

I go to lift her from the floor and she flinches. I tell her, "It's okay, it's fine." I lead her to the sink and wash the blood from her hands in the warm tap water. I tell her nobody is going to hurt her. Martini glasses are replaceable.

"Oh daddy," she says.

I wash her hands and watch the blood mix with the water and circle the white porcelain sink. I talk to her about nothing in particular. Our elusive dirty martini. "The secret of the dirty martini is olive brine but not much of it," I say. Brine will give the martini an opaque color and a salty and bittersweet taste. I tell her at times she will wish the martini had more clarity. She will wish she could see straight through to the olive. But Nothing is perfect.

A Beggar's Life

He was drinking his third glass of red and waiting for her at the Gran Café Roma. Waiters wore starched white bib aprons, and the small tables were outside and covered in yellow linen. The ends of the cloth flicked this way and that with the breeze. He did not want her anymore, that's what he pictured himself telling her. You see nothing beyond yourself, Sylvia. They were done, more than done.

Martin liked sitting outside to drink. Everything tasted better outside. He liked to roll the glass stem between his fingers and breathe in the fragrance of the wine. A fruity smell, a woody smell, whatever might be there. Martin had long thin fingers and his nails were manicured. Sylvia thought he had pretty hands. You have such feminine hands, she would say.

The leaves of the birch trees on the Via Veneto were yellow and frosted lime and red, and the trunks were pale gray and charcoal. Leaves covered the sidewalk. Leaves collected on the round café tables. The colors looked bright against the white tablecloths and the sunny streets. Fumes from motor bikes and buses mixed with the smell of frying meat and fish. Martin loved Rome and he loved it best in autumn.

Only the old beggar women annoyed Martin. They were short with small feet and thick bodies. They wore black dresses that covered their arms and their black square toed shoes. Black scarves draped their hair and faces. The old women would get down on their knees and lower their foreheads to the gray sidewalk. They liked to shake and pretend to cry. They held up pictures of Jesus with His bleeding heart.

Aiuti la misericordia difficile del ritrovamento, they would chant. Help the poor find mercy. *Aiuti i poor vivono questa vita*. Help the poor live this life.

They expected you to drop coins into the tin cans beside them. Martin refused to give them coins, he had vowed never to do that. One evening last month he got so upset with an old woman who was begging near the café that he threw her tin can and her coins across the street. He was drunk and obsessing about Sylvia. His Sylvia had dark hair and perfect teeth and pale endless legs. After Martin had thrown the old beggar woman's tin can and coins across the street, he felt ashamed and had given the woman fifty euros but she kept her forehead to the sidewalk and continued to shake and cry as though he wasn't there.

A pack of motorcyclists on the Via Veneto passed by Martin. The men were dressed in dark suits and colorful ties and the women wore high heels and their skirts fluttered about their legs. Everybody had gray or black helmets. Some of the riders were smoking cigarettes. They zigzagged about the cars and buses.

Martin watched the traffic and sipped his wine. Roman traffic was different than New York traffic. It was a fast and silent dance. They were used to it, and the motorcyclists had no expressions. The rule was to get where you were going.

What did the old woman ever do to you? Sylvia had written this in an email. Did she steal from you? Did she threaten you?

Martin remembered looking at her words on his computer screen. He had emailed Sylvia while he was home in New York and confessed to tossing the old beggar woman's coins across the street. Sylvia had emailed him back with questions. Martin worked for an accounting firm that did European bank audits. This is how he had met Sylvia. She was an accountant at one of the banks he audited. He traveled to Italy every other month. February, April, June, that sort of thing. He never answered Sylvia's questions. Martin had walked into the downstairs bathroom and vomited. He could hear his wife calling to him from the kitchen. Martin? she said. Martin, are you all right?

A yellow leaf from a nearby birch tree landed on his table. He was rolling the stem of his wine glass between his thumb and slender forefinger, and he stared at the leaf as if it were an intruder.

What Martin had first noticed about Rome were the trees. Pines rose above the city like tall mushrooms with scaly brown trunks. Cedars filled Borghese Park and the hills and lined some of the streets. Boxwood and palms had rooted together. These trees seemed like strangers to one another, that was Martin's thought. They had nothing in common but soil and circumstance.

The chanting had started again. *Aiuti una donna anziana a trovare la misericordia*, she was saying. Help an old woman find mercy. Then she said, *Aiuti i poor vivono questa vita.* Help the poor live this life. Martin heard her behind him and glanced over his shoulder. Another old beggar woman laid face down on the gray sidewalk and the bright autumn leaves. She was small and heavy like the first beggar but they all chanted similar things and Martin didn't think she was the old woman who had made him angry. Who knew, really? A black dress covered her arms and legs. A black scarf hid her face. She shook her body and moaned like the other old woman. He couldn't escape the beggars. Martin had seen the old women in the Piazza di Spagna and the market square of Campo de Fiori. He had seen them outside the Colosseum and the Piazza San Pietro and the Pantheon, any place tourists gathered. The old women laid face down on ground with their bamboo canes and their pictures of Jesus. They laid like rumpled shadows on the gray sidewalks and cobblestones.

"How long have you been doing this?" his wife said. Barb had listened in on one of his telephone calls to Rome. Four o'clock that morning and they were downstairs in his study. A silver desk lamp gave a small circle of light to the dark room. She wore her pink terry cloth robe. Her thin shoulders were trembling and her fingers worked the back of her short hair.

"Tell me," she said. "I'm curious, Martin, okay? Just tell me how long you've been screwing some other woman in some other country."

"I don't know, "he said. His upper lip kept sticking on his dry teeth. "Six months," he said. "More, less, I don't know."

Martin did keep track. Six months, four days, and eleven hours, that's how long. There were days he could have told his wife how long in minutes.

"We have children," Barb said. Her eyes had gone glassy and wet. Then she said, "What's wrong with you? You betrayed me. A fifteen year marriage and you do this? You betrayed your own children."

"I love my children," he said.

"And me?" She didn't look at him when she said it.

"I don't know," he said. Neither one of them had known that for years. He couldn't remember the last time they had used the word love without referring to the children.

THE TWO YOUNG women had expensive jeans and knee high boots and silk scarves wrapped about their necks. Their colors varied but the outfits were the same. They sat a table away from Martin at the café. They were tall and thin and pretty, the sort of pretty you saw dressed in the Missoni fashion magazines, the long crinkly hair, the cheekbones that could cut you. Both women smoked cigarettes while they talked.

Their Italian was too fast for Martin to understand. The cigarettes were held between their long fingers and red polished nails. Smoke trailed the motion of their hands.

He had missed Sylvia bad enough to take chances, phone calls at three and four in the morning, gifts using his credit card, leaving a photograph of her in the top drawer of his desk at home, wearing the jeans and sport shirts she had given him, the platinum ID bracelet with their names engraved on the back. He was a criminal looking for the cops.

Four months had passed since his divorce from Barb. Martin still missed Sylvia when he was in New York. He missed her far too much. Martin missed her the way hungry teenagers miss each other.

"We should take it easy," Sylvia had said at the beginning of everything. She was laying naked beside him in their room at the Empire Palace on the Via Aureliana. The down on her upper thigh was gold from the sunlight. She said, "You have your wife and I have my friends. We can see each other when you come to Roma. Be together. Si? We can keep it light, keep it fun."

"That's what they do in Roma?" he said. "Is light and fun the thing you do?"

"You don't like fun?" she said.

"Fun is okay," he said. "I'm not against fun."

"We have no worries with light and fun," Sylvia had said.

"No worries," he said.

Martin started to like light and fun less and less. Then he

didn't like it at all. He didn't like calling her at three or four in the morning and hearing Sylvia giggle at all the things he wasn't saying or doing.

"Who's there with you?" he had said. "What is that noise?"

"When are you coming to Roma?" she said.

"Answer my question," he said.

"How is Barbara?" Sylvia wanted to know.

All right, Martin thought, I have Barbara. I have my children. I have a home in a beautiful neighborhood. It's unfair to expect Sylvia to throw away her life and wait for someone who already has a life.

"Who is there with you?" Martin was still saying this after his divorce. "What noise?" He said this after Barbara was gone from his life and he could that only see his two children every other weekend and one month in the summer.

"When are you coming to Roma?" she said. Her voice was tight and distant.

Martin hated these phone calls but he couldn't stop it. Each call left him with a paranoid feeling and an unchanging truth. This wasn't about Martin being married or not being married or whether he was in Rome or New York. Sylvia was going to do what Sylvia was going to do. That was her life, her mantra. Neither Martin or keeping things light and fun mattered.

THE WAITER HAD just brought Martin a fourth glass of red. Waiters had their own pace and rules here. Everyone had to order something and everyone had a long time to eat and drink whatever they had ordered. Martin sipped the wine then glanced at his watch. Sylvia had promised to meet him at the café at one o'clock and it was now two fifteen. Lunch had come and gone. His shoulders had started to ache.

The old beggar woman had started up, and Martin could hear her somewhere behind him. *Aiuti la misericordia difficile del ritrovamento*, she was chanting. Help the poor find mercy. Over and over, didn't she ever tire of it?

He was wearing Sylvia's presents today, the platinum ID bracelet that had their names engraved on the back, the jeans fashionably torn at the thigh and knee.

Martin was still waiting for Sylvia and working on his fourth glass of red and watching a smiling old man two tables away. The old man had his suitcoat draped over his shoulders. Italian men never use the sleeves of their suitcoats. He had big sunglasses and slicked back white hair and shiny thin shoes. The old man sat at the table closest to the sidewalk. He would raise his wine glass to the young women who passed by him. He raised his glass to the ugly ones and the pretty ones, it made no difference.

"WHAT ARE YOU doing here?" Sylvia had said that to Martin late last night when he showed up at her apartment near Borghese Park on the Via Pinciana. Her dark hair was tangled from sleep and she clutched her silk pink and silver robe at the neck.

"You should invite me in and I'll tell you," Martin said. He could barely steady his breath.

"You need to call first," she said. Her eyes were half-closed and her voice was clotty from sleep.

"Oh, come on, Sylvia," he said. He tried to see past the half open door. "I've missed you, for God sake. I miss you all the time."

"We can talk tomorrow," Sylvia said. She yawned and covered her open mouth with her red fingernails. "We can have lunch. Okay? You call tomorrow.

Maybe ten, ten thirty. Okay?"

"Didn't you miss me?" Martin said. He hated hearing himself pout. Despised it, really. "Six hours on a plane," he said, "and I couldn't think of anything or anyone but you. I don't get it. I can't believe you didn't miss me."

"Of course, I missed you," she said but he could tell she was already tired of the conversation. "I missed you very much," she said. "I always miss you."

"*Chie e esso?*" a man's voice said. Who is it? He was hidden by the door.

"Who is that?" Martin said to Sylvia.

"I don't want to explain myself," she said.

"Who is that?" Martin said again.

"Is it your American?" the Italian man said behind the door.

"We can talk tomorrow," Sylvia said to Martin.

"Who the hell is that?" Martin said.

"Light and fun," she said and shook a finger at him.

"For who?" he said.

AFTERNOON SUNSHINE WENT through the branches and the leaves of the birch trees and covered the white linen table cloth with light and shadows. Sunshine reflected off Martin's empty wine glass. Red and yellow and lime green leaves laid about the thin wooden legs of the tables and on the gray sidewalk. Martin looked at his watch. She was almost three hours late. He still wanted to think of her as a woman who kept her word. He had pictured Sylvia appearing promptly at one o'clock. Her dark hair would be pulled back, a long white leather coat snitched at her slim waste, her mirror sunglasses concealing weary but vigilant eyes.

Martin pulled a twenty and a five from the front pocket of his jeans and slipped the euros under the empty wine glass. He stood and held onto the table. The birch trees on the Via Veneto blurred and turned. The motorbikes and the buses and the cars blurred and turned, too. Martin steadied himself then began to walk. The old beggar woman was four or five yards away. She laid face down on the gray sidewalk and shook her upper body and showed her picture of Jesus with His big red heart. Martin imagined kneeling next to the old woman and grabbing the back of her thick neck and shaking her. Quit this, he would shout at her. Aren't you ashamed? he would say.

The right heel of his boot caught a break in the sidewalk. His ankle bent to the left and he fell hard on his right knee. His skin scraped the pavement at the opening of his already torn jeans. The pain from his ankle and his bloodied knee surprised him. He shut his eyes tight but couldn't stop the tears. Martin rolled to one side and gripped his leg.

"Do you know what time it is?" Sylvia had said that morning.

"It's ten," Martin said. "You told me to call you at ten."

"Don't you sleep?" Sylvia said. She lighted a cigarette and exhaled the smoke into the receiver of her cell phone. Then she said, "What is it, Martin? What do you want?"

"I'm checking on lunch," he said. His voice was too tight and too anxious but he couldn't make it different. "You told me we'd have lunch. So I thought, the Gran Café Roma. You know, where we first had lunch."

"That's such a tourist trap, "she said

"You told me you loved it," he said.

Sylvia sighed and exhaled more smoke from her cigarette. "I guess I need to talk to you," she said.

"What do you mean talk to me?" Martin wanted to know.

"Talk to you," she said.

Well I need to talk to you, he had thought.

Martin was still lying on the gray sidewalk. He gripped his bloody leg and tried to rub the swelling from his ankle. As soon as the pain stopped he was going to open his eyes and go over to the old beggar woman. He wanted to apologize. He wanted to shake her. Something. Anything. You should stop this life, he wanted to tell her.

What Fire Does

"Fire sticks to the skin and won't let you go." This was how her mother explained what happened to Carlyle's face. Her mother was a worn and fragile looking woman named Greta. Her eyes were gentle and dark and she liked to study you a second or two before she talked. "Fire can take the chill or get mean like it did with Carlyle. Fire can cook you the way steak burns black and sweet on the grill. It can hurt you so bad you don't hurt at all," Greta said. Her hands were bones and cherry red polish, and the long fingers had a tremble. "Fire can burn the feelings off your skin. The feelings come back soon enough but when they do come back you will wish they had gone somewhere else." Then her mother said, "I don't blame Carlyle, hon. The boy needed to leave."

Taye had her tenth birthday last Saturday. This afternoon she is riding the bus down Granby Street by herself to visit her father. She hasn't seen him in two years and her stomach feels knotted. Only Carlyle knows about her plan to visit her father and he does not like the idea. Pink and white Crape Myrtles line the median and blossoms are scattered over mowed grass that separate the trees. Taye is leaning her head against the black plastic seat next to the window. She closes her eyes. Taye can feel the sun warm her cheeks and forehead. The thick summer air has the smell of exhaust fumes from the traffic. Taye wants to straighten everything out between Carlyle and their father. Howard the Furious, that's Carlyle's name for him. Now that she is older maybe Howard the Furious will listen.

Taye remembers when Carlyle first painted her toenails. She was five and her brother was fifteen. They sat on her double bed with the dark wood posts and the white canopy. Stuffed animals laid about the pillows. Rabbits and bears, mostly. Sunlight stretched across the quilted bedspread. All three windows were open and brought the scent of boxwood into the room. Greta once told Taye there were more boxwood and Crape Myrtle in Virginia than just about anywhere. That was especially true in Norfolk.

"Hold still," Carlyle said. He had wedged a cotton ball between each of her toes.

Her brother pushed his clear plastic framed glasses up the ridge of his nose. The glasses had white adhesive tape on both the bridge and the right temple. His face was close to her bare foot, his skinny tan legs tucked under him.

Taye felt his breath touching her skin.

"You're tickling," Taye said. She tilted her head to see what sort of job he was doing. She said, "I have pink toes."

"Flamingo Pink," Carlyle said and tried to steady her small foot.

"I have Flamingo Pink toes," Taye said.

Carlyle and Taye favored Greta. They were both thin with dark hair and their eyes were set deep and shadowed. Carlyle was six or seven inches taller than his sister. He had a graceful, lazy stride. Taye thought he walked like someone being carried on a breeze. She told him that once and Carlyle shrugged his shoulders as if to say, what can you do?

HALFWAY THROUGH SUPPER Taye had lifted her thin bare leg above the table and wiggled her Flamingo Pink toes and said to everyone, "Look here. Look at this. Carlyle painted my toes. Go ahead Carlyle, tell mama and daddy how you painted my beautiful toes."

Carlyle hadn't said anything. He wasn't listening, or that's how Taye saw it. Carlyle was smearing butter on a roll with the back of his fork.

Her mother told Taye that she needed to take her beautiful toes off the table. Greta had lighted two candles earlier and placed them atop a brocaded linen cloth. The candles were in silver holders. The room smelled of roast chicken and dinner rolls made from scratch. There was also the smell of flowers and damp grass coming through the screen door. Yellow candlelight quivered along the white walls. The light made shadows in the corners.

Greta looked at Howard. Her long fingers played with a linen napkin. Cherry red nails poked about like nervous insects. Howard didn't look at Greta.

He was cutting a piece of chicken breast and staring down at his plate. Howard had big shoulders and big arms and hands. His face was broad and pock marked from bad years with acne. The bristle about his jaw and chin would not grow into a beard and his rust colored hair would not stay combed. Howard liked being outdoors and doing dangerous things. He started working for the Norfolk fire department before his children were born. Howard wasn't much of a talker. He had once told Carlyle that people didn't listen to a man who talked too much.

A CLOWN IS a mystery. Carlyle said that to Taye yesterday afternoon. He was dressed as a clown and making balloon animals in the city park for a group of pre-schoolers. Carlyle was living with Greta's mother in Gent, an area close to downtown Norfolk. Taye had never seen her brother's scarred face, what the fire had done. He was still wearing bandages and going through surgeries when he left home to live with their grandmother. She did not see the scars yesterday, either. His face was painted white and his mouth was shaped into a red smile. The lips were exaggerated ear to ear. Carlyle also had a red plastic nose and his eyebrows were thick black arcs.

"A Clown can go any place and nobody will know him," Carlyle said. "It's my perfect disguise. Then he had said, "Criminals dress up as clowns to escape the police. Did you know that, Taye? A lot of criminals do it. They dress up as clowns and rob banks and gas stations. But the smarter criminals dress up as clowns after they rob the banks. That way the police won't know them and they can get good jobs and have friends. Clowns can get away with anything, Taye. They can get away with living their lives."

THE BUS BACKFIRES once and shakes as the driver shifts gears. Taye is on her knees in the black plastic seat. She watches as Granby High School passes her window. Large oaks and maples shade a front lawn that is gray dirt and spotty islands of grass. Magnolias with white blossoms are behind two low brick walls. The walls converge to a wide concrete sidewalk and the school's main entrance way. Taye's bus is shaking its way toward Ward's Corner where her father has an apartment.

Greta once told Taye that boys fight all the time. Carlyle hadn't been in a single fight until Granby High. Then every couple of weeks he seemed to have an ice pack on his lip or his nose. One eye or the other stayed swollen. His clear plastic glasses were held together with a piece of white adhesive tape on the bridge and the right temple.

"A bloody nose, a bruised eye, nobody's talking the end of the world, Greta would say. "Okay, baby? This isn't a major ordeal. You let me take care of Carlyle," that's what Greta would say. Her mother's face had a gaunt, worn look. She would say, "I thought you kids were so accepting of one another. Whatever happened to that? Can you tell me, please?"

Taye was five then. She had skinny arms and legs and that same gaunt look as her mother.

"Are you angry at me?" Taye said.

"No, baby," Greta said and hugged her daughter and kissed her forehead. Tears appeared on the rims of Greta's eyes.

"Are you sad?" Taye wanted to know.

"Not because of you," her mother said.

Now Taye is ten and she likes telling her mother what Carlyle had told her. Some people accept you and some people slap you around.

"CARLYLE WAS A handsome boy," Greta said. "Handsome in a very pretty way. You know, pretty girl features. The fire took the right side of his face and most of his upper lip. Scarred his body, too. His pretty skin just seemed to melt away." Finally her mother said, "Fire can get you too cautious. You can't live your life without thinking and plotting. After a fire like that you have to keep two moves ahead of yourself. Will this get me in trouble, you think. If I do so and so, will that come back later and hurt me?" Her mother had said this to Taye when she was trying to explain Carlyle's reclusive behavior. "All the hiding out," she said. "The way you have to disguise yourself to fool the flames and cover the scars." Greta was the one who told her that Carlyle was making balloon animals at birthday parties. "Do you think he wants to do that?" her mother said. "Do you think Carlyle likes to paint his face with white grease and put on a big red smile? That's the fire talking, Taye. That's what the fire does. You spend most of your time hiding the damage and watching your back. It compromises you. It scares you out of living."

TAYE CAN SEE Ward's Corner from the window of the Granby Street bus. There is a big music store on the corner with bright yellow and blue walls and lots of chrome and glass. There are two sub shops and an Italian restaurant near the music store. The Italian restaurant is called il Sorrento and has a neon sign of a man steering his gondola. The man wears a straw hat with a red ribbon. Across the street, Cole's Apparel displays shoes at fifty percent off and dresses reduced by a third to make room for the new fall fashions. A multiplex cinema has an optometrist store to its right and an insurance/bail bondsman to its left. Next to the bondsman is an electronics store that advertises the best deals on flat screen TVs in Norfolk. At a diagonal corner is the new Maxi Drug with a drive thru prescription window.

HOWARD THE FURIOUS lives in the apartment complex a block behind the department store on Fayton Avenue. The apartments are old with dark brown bricks and trimmed boxwood and shady trees along the curbs. Taye and her brother have walked by their father's apartment more than once but they have never stopped to visit. The street has the smell of honeysuckle in the summer. Yesterday in the park Taye told her brother how she was going to visit Howard the Furious and make things better for everybody.

Taye remembers laying on Carlyle's bed and watching her brother line his eyes with a black pencil in front of a mirror. Taye was six then and thought her brother should be a movie star. His eyelids were painted glittery silver and his cheeks and lips had a pale red color. Carlyle also wore eyelashes that came from a box. Taye thought the eyelashes were caterpillars. After Carlyle finished dressing he walked and turned for Taye like a model. He had on a black dress that showed his slim figure and black high heels and a blond wig. The hair was straight and ended past his shoulders. Taye leaped up and down on Carlyle's bed and clapped.

This was when Harold the Furious walked into Carlyle's room. Her father hadn't said anything. He mostly yelled at everybody but this time Harold and Carlyle just looked at each other. Taye stopped jumping on the bed and watched them. She couldn't tell what her father was feeling or thinking. He didn't have an expression. Harold the Furious smelled of cigarette smoke and old sweat.

"Look at Carlyle's eyelashes," Taye said and pointed to her brother. "Aren't they beautiful, daddy? Carlyle's eyelashes come in a box."

"I woke up with fire on me." That's what Carlyle said to

her yesterday in the park. He had just finished making balloon animals for the pre-schoolers. Carlyle was dressed in his clown suit with the silver baggy pants and the long funny feet. His face was white and he had red lips that went from ear to ear.

"I opened my eyes," Carlyle said, "and I knew my face was on fire. I didn't feel anything, not right away. But I knew the flames were on my face. I knew the tent was burning, and I could see the overturned Kerosene lantern. I had to roll in the dirt to put out the fire."

Carlyle stopped talking and watched the children in the park. He wasn't wearing his clear plastic glasses. Taye wondered if he could see. Pre-schoolers ran on the newly cut grass and among the trees. Some of the pre-schoolers held their balloon animals as they ran. The air was warm and had the smell of pine and flowers.

Their father had taken Carlyle camping in the Blue Ridge a month or so after he walked into the bedroom and saw Carlyle wearing makeup and a blond wig. This is what Greta told Taye. Taye also heard the story when the police came to talk to her mother. Carlyle and Taye had gone camping many times but always with both parents, the whole family.

"Who knows what was on his mind," Carlyle said, meaning his father. "Daddy probably had the idea that father- son camping would stop me from buying cosmetics. I always adored the Blue Ridge. Believe it or not, I liked camping with Howard the Furious. That whole father-son thing terrified and thrilled me."

Carlyle stopped talking again. He looked down at his big brown clown shoes. The soles and tops were split in the front like crocodile mouths. He tapped the toes of the shoes together and smiled to himself. Taye thought the smile didn't look happy.

Their father had been sipping vodka from a silver flask that night in the Blue Ridge. The sky had a half moon and stars. A small waterfall and stream were nearby and Carlyle could hear the water rush over the rocks, the sounds of insects, and an owl. Tall birch trees and pine cut the moonlight. The smell of wet earth and canvas was strong in the tent.

"I didn't think much about the drinking," Carlyle had said. "Daddy liked to drink when he went camping. But this time he seemed angry. I heard him outside somewhere just before I fell asleep. He was cursing and talking to himself."

The police told Greta what they thought had happened. Their theory, they said. A pretty safe bet, they said. The police figured Howard got drunk and worked up and threw the Kerosene lantern into the tent and then passed out. Howard swore he did not remember anything. Norfolk General District Court gave him a year's suspended jail time and a rehabilitation program for his drinking. Greta gave him a divorce.

TAYE LEAVES THE Granby Street bus at Ward's Corner in front of Cole's Apparel. The afternoon is hot and sunlight reflects off the sidewalk. Taye has on her sunglasses but still squints her eyes. Her legs and arms are tanned and skinny. She wears knee-length pink shorts and pink high tops and a white t-shirt. Exhaust fumes from the traffic make the air feel thick and smell of gasoline.

When Taye reaches Fayton Avenue everything becomes cool and shady. Taye is feeling anxious and her stomach has started to get crampy. Just because she is ten now doesn't mean Howard the Furious is going to listen. There are no guarantees, she thinks. Her mother always tells her that. But Taye wants her family. She wants her father and Carlyle to love each other or at least like each other. Greta also says people have to try.

Fayton Avenue is part of an old neighborhood. Big oaks and maples line both curbs. The branches on the tree tops are heavy enough to sag into an archway that stops the sunlight from reaching the gravel street. Only tiny needles of light get through the branches and leaves. The sidewalk is lumpy and cracked from the tree roots. Trimmed boxwood surround each apartment complex. The buildings are all dark brown bricks. Her father lives in the last complex on the right, the one called Spotswood Manor.

"Let's go home, Taye." It's Carlyle voice.

She hears him before she sees him. And when she sees him, she doesn't see all of him. Carlyle is sitting behind the steering wheel of a gray pickup truck parked by the curb. Shadows hide his face and the right side of his upper body. Both windows are rolled down to let in the warm air. The truck looks old but clean. The right front fender has rusted. Carlyle slides over to the passenger's side.

Taye is watching a crack in the sidewalk. She remembers being at the park yesterday with Carlyle. Clowns can get away with anything, Taye. That's what her brother had said to her. They can get away with living their lives. He is letting her see under the bandages and the white face and the red clown lips for the first time. He is doing this for me, Taye thinks, and knows it can't be easy. Taye isn't sure she wants him to give up his disguise.

"Look at my face," Carlyle says. "Look at what Howard the Furious did, Taye. Look at everything. If you want to scream, you go on and do it, you go right ahead. But before you see Howard, you have to look at me. I want you to, okay? I love you so much, Taye. And I want you to look."

Carlyle opens the passenger door. He is wearing wrinkled chinos and brown loafers without socks and a baby blue V-neck sweater. His hair is crayon blond with dark roots and combed straight back. He has on his clear plastic glasses with the white adhesive tape wrapped about the bridge and the right temple.

Taye glances up at Carlyle then back at the crack in the sidewalk.

"You should buy new glasses," she says.

"High school memories," Carlyle says. He says this like it's the punchline of a joke.

Taye is looking at him now. Carlyle's left cheek is drawn together, wrinkled and fleshy. Most of his upper lip is gone. His white even teeth and upper gum are visible. The right side of his head is smooth and pink and shiny. The rim of his right ear and lobe are burned away, the same for his right nostril. His nose is bunched at the tip like pressed on clay. The edge of his right eyebrow and the corner of his right eye have been fused together. The V of his baby blue cotton sweater framed other pink irregular folds, other tiny craters of skin. Scars are on his throat and perhaps his chest and stomach, perhaps his arms and his legs. Taye did not want to know. Taye did not want see anymore skin. She looked down at the crack in the sidewalk.

"I don't like it, either," Carlyle says. His thin fingers touch the smooth pink side of his head. He says, "I don't like seeing it or showing it. I don't know, what else can you do?" Then Carlyle pats the beige and brown plaid seat and says, "Come on and let's go home."

Taye climbs into the truck and buckles her safety harness.

"Maybe daddy's sorry," Taye says.

"Being sorry today is easy," Carlyle says and turns the key in the ignition. The engine starts right up, and he shifts into first. Carlyle says, "With people like Howard the Furious, you have to worry about tomorrow."

Shadows and sunlight go across the hood of the truck. Her brother watches the road. He has one hand on the steering wheel, an arm propped on the rim of the open window. His aftershave smells of cinnamon and lime.

The truck moves down Fayton Avenue toward Granby Street and the bright afternoon sun. An archway of branches and leaves sways above their truck. Taye leans her head against the beige and brown plaid seat and looks at her brother. She had a birthday last Saturday and she is older now. Taye studies her brother's face. Taye studies his scars and the sunlight on them and the shadows that pass over them.

Little Gypsies

They were stoning her, two boys and three girls. The bunch couldn't have been older than nine or ten, and that included the girl being stoned. Horace watched them and did nothing, not at first. At first he wanted to spin what he was seeing into something he could live with. Didn't children like to pretend? You be this and I'll be that. Children pretended all the time, didn't they? When he saw blood, the argument left him.

Horace was standing near the church of San Trovaso beside the canal. He had hiked there from San Marco, crossing the Ponte dell' Accademia, completely lost but enjoying the warm Venetian night. Forty-two years ago, he and his wife, Celeste, had come to Venice for their honeymoon. He was in his early sixties now, still slim, still barely graying. His wife had died last month after a two year battle with a carcinoma the size of a soccer ball.

The girl lay on the cobblestone, her skinny knees pressed to her chest, her hands buried in her dark tangled hair. Blood seeped between her fingers. Horace shouted at the children. He said, *"Arresto! Arresti questio immediatamente!"* Stop! Stop this at once! A boy with black eyes and thin dirty legs threw a stone at Horace, grazing the side of his forehead. Horace felt a sting and a warm liquid down his left temple and knew he was bleeding. Now the three girls and the other boy began throwing stones at him. They were yelling in a language he did not understand. Horace used his forearm to protect his face. He knelt and picked up a handful of smaller stones and began throwing them at the two boys and the three girls. Again, he shouted at them. He said, *"Esca! Esca!"* Get out! Get out!

Horace used a folded white linen handkerchief to wipe the blood and the dirt from the girl's face. He smelled sweat and urine on her. She said her name was Tusia and that she lived near Rome. Her English was better than his patchy Italian.

Tusia told him why the children were stoning her. She said, "I take their money. Money they steal from tourists."

"Good for you," Horace said. "Were you giving it back to the tourists?"

"No, keep it," she said.

Tusia couldn't stay conscious, and Horace carried her to a water taxi and told the driver to get them to the doctor.

He was holding the unconscious child with both arms as they entered the hospital at Campo Santi Giovanni, her head propped on his shoulder. She weighed nothing, just bones and air. How did a person this small and light remain on the ground? Why didn't she just sail off like a balloon? Her face had tiny features, tiny nose, tiny mouth, her skin pale against her dark tangled hair.

Nurses and orderlies walked past Horace as if he and the girl weren't there. He began shouting at them, too. *"Chiamici un medico!"* he said. *"Dove e' il medico?"* Get us a doctor! Where is the doctor? That was when Tusia opened her eyes halfway and looked up at Horace. She had large brown eyes the color of fall acorns.

A young orderly with short black hair and a thick mustache started to lift Tusia onto a gurney but her arms locked about Horace's neck. Skin had been scraped from both her elbows, the dried blood already beginning to scab.

"Don't leave Tusia. Okay?" she said. "Sir, stay with Tusia."

HORACE HAD BOUGHT his wife a twenty lira gold coin on a gold chain during their honeymoon. Forty-two years and Celeste never took the pendent from her neck. She had showered with it, slept with it, and went about her life with it. When she died, Horace removed the coin while she laid in her coffin at the funeral home. Whatever pants he wore on whatever day, the gold coin and chain were always in his front pocket. He loved touching it. He loved to rub the coin and chain between his forefinger and thumb like worry beads.

"They hide on the treni, si?" Dr. Golemba said to Horace. Then he said, "Ecuse, I mean trains. They hide on trains."

Horace rubbed the gold coin in the front pocket of his tan gabardines as he listened to the doctor.

Dr. Golemba was slender and delicate with long pale fingers and thinning black hair slicked straight back. He had finished putting six stitches in Tusia's scalp and three stitches beneath her left eye. He had also cleaned her scraped skin and bandaged her elbows, knees, and her right shoulder. Dr. Golemba was talking to Horace in the waiting room, explaining the little gypsies.

"They come from the south on the trains to steal," the doctor said. "That's what they do. They come here to Venezia to steal. They are professionisti, si? Very, very. The parents teach them. What can you do? They call themselves the Romani, the Roma. That's what they want you to call them, the Roma."

Horace was listening to Dr. Golemba but thinking about Celeste. When his wife called her doctor, she had talked to the woman who scheduled appointments.

"No, it's not an emergency," Celeste said. "I just don't feel like myself."

"We have an April 3rd at 3:30," the woman said. "That's the earliest he's got. If it was an emergency, he could see you sooner. You're sure it isn't an emergency?"

Celeste hated bothering people, so she waited the two months. By that time the tumor in her abdominal cavity had grown from five and a half centimeters to twenty-six centimeters and was siphoning her blood supply. The tumor pressed against the bottom of her stomach and its weight and its hunger fatigued her and hurt her back. When Dr. Michie opened Celeste and saw the size the of tumor and the number of vessels that ran through it, he closed her and went to plan B.

"Are you all right, sir?" Dr. Golemba said.

"Tusia told me she's from Rome," Horace said.

He didn't like being in hospitals. They smelled like cleaning chemicals and reminded him of how his wife suffered with her treatment. Hospitals left him feeling helpless and angry.

"Si, outside the city," Dr. Golemba said. "Many Roma outside the city. Very poor, very dirty. The parents send the children into the streets to steal. The children, they are like lupi with the tourists, like the wolves, si? These little gypsies, they wait in the train stations, the ruins. *Li circondano.* How you say? They surround our tourists. The Americans, the Dutch, the Japanese, it doesn't matter. The children show them paper signs. The tourist, they try to read. This is when the little gypsies surround them and steal."

Dr. Michie had smiled and sat next to Celeste's bed.

"We'll do chemo," Dr. Michie had said to Celeste and Horace. Dr. Michie liked using the royal we. "We can't remove the tumor now, it's dug itself in," he'd said. "We don't want any hemorrhaging, do we? The prudent way is to shrink it."

Shrinking the tumor would take six eight hour sessions. Celeste had a small hole drilled into her upper chest for a Port-a-cath which was inserted into a vessel near her heart.

The chemicals kill everything. They don't know the

difference between good tissue and cancerous tissue. The chemicals are nondenominational killers.

Celeste once told Horace, "If the cancer doesn't get me, the treatment will."

"Don't talk that way," Horace said. "You shouldn't put that sort of thought out there. I hate when you talk like that. You'll be fine, you'll be more than fine." Horace and Celeste had been together since they were kids, since high school. He touched her cheek with his palm. She had a smooth tranquil face with green-gray eyes that always approved of him. Horace said, "It's unbelievable. You're still a beauty, you know that? How can you have no hair and still be a beauty? Answer me that one."

HORACE WAS IN the bedroom of his second floor apartment on the Ghetto Vecchio, staring out the open window. He liked the Jewish Quarter, the shady piazza, the ancient synagogues. He and Celeste had rented this same apartment on their honeymoon, far too many years ago now. They had eaten early dinners at the little the kosher bar and restaurant near the Ponte delle Guglie.

"Sir lucky to live here," Tusia said. Her voice was thick and whispery from sleep. She lay in the bed with her head and her shoulders raised, leaning against a stack of three pillows. White gauze hid the left side of her face, the skin bruised, swollen, and both elbows and her right shoulder were bandaged. While she was in the hospital the orderlies had bathed her and shampooed and brushed her dark hair. Horace's double bed made the child appear even smaller and thinner than she'd looked lying in the street. Then Tusia said, "Do I stay here? Does Tusia stay with Sir? I cook and clean. I am good cook, Sir, you'll see."

Horace thought the girl spoke better English than Dr. Golemba, but Dr. Golemba didn't have to forage the tourists for food.

"All I want you to do is rest," Horace said. "I'm going to give you some antibiotics. When you're well, you can go back to Rome. Will your parents be worried? Should I call them?"

"I live with my sister," Tusia said and gave a weak and dismissive wave of her hand. "Her boyfriend happy Tusia gone. I stay with you; I be your little girl. Such a beautiful apartamento."

The apartment wasn't beautiful. Tusia thought it was beautiful because of where and how she lived, Horace knew that. He was no different than she when it came to this place. The beauty here had nothing to do with the apartment and everything to do with the memory of his Celeste. Its marble floor and high ceiling were lost to the peeling and cracked beige walls and the cheap furniture. The walls needed scraping. They needed new plaster and paint.

"My wife and I stayed here on our honeymoon," Horace said. He sat at the edge of the black wrought iron bed and held the girl's thin hand. He said, "My wife died last month but we had many good years." Horace tried to sound upbeat. "I filled this apartment with wonderful flowers and brought her here blindfolded. We were both very young, and the apartment and the flowers were a surprise. My wife was so happy she cried. I remember that, the crying. You should have seen her."

"I bet she was a pretty wife," Tusia said and adjusted the bed sheet about her waist. She wore a white cotton nightgown with a brocade collar and short sleeves. Horace bought the gown yesterday on their way back from the hospital. Tusia smiled, her swollen, bruised lips keeping the smile only for a moment. She said, "You know why Tusia think Sir had a pretty wife? Pretty wives like the handsome husband."

"I'm leaving at the end of the summer," Horace said. He gave her two blue and white pills from the plastic bottle on the nightstand and a paper cup of water. He watched her swallow the pills and return the cup to the nightstand. Horace wanted to keep his upbeat tone. "You, Miss Tusia, you'll be ready to leave in the next couple of weeks, after your stitches come out." he said. "I'm sure you won't have trouble finding tourists to charm."

THIS MORNING HORACE forgot the pain. He had been using his living room sofa as a bed and the foam-worn cushions were working bad magic on his lower back He called the impromptu bed his Roy Rogers sofa, a brown and green plaid that had found its way into Venice but belonged in a bunk house. Horace slipped on his navy blue terry cloth robe and glanced about the apartment. He was sleepy and squinting his eyes, not ready for the sunlight. This morning the living room, kitchen, and bed room were filled with flowers.

"Surprise," Tusia said. She grinned and covered that grin with her hand.

"God, what have you done?" Horace said Look at these flowers. Tears smeared his vision. Memories and sadness swelled his chest. There were bright vases of white and pink roses, orange gerberas, purple and white gladiolas, yellow lilies and sunflowers. Horace felt he had awakened inside a cloud of color. He said, "I don't want to ask how you did it."

"You like my surprise?" Tusia said.

"How did you do it?"

"See, I make Sir happy."

Horace had taken Tusia back to the hospital two days ago. Her stitches and bandages were gone. Yellowish bruises tinted the left side of her face and her right shoulder. Tiny black dots where the stitches had been curved beneath her left eye.

"I stay with Sir," Tusia said. "Summer go, I go. Okay? Good deal? I cook and clean."

Horace stared at the black and white marble floor and didn't answer. Maybe he should not have helped the child at all, that was what he thought. Then he tried to think of a kinder way to tell her what he had already told her.

"Your stitches are out now," Horace said. He was still staring at the marble floor. "Now its time for you to go. That was our arrangement." Horace looked up at her. He wanted to smile and be upbeat but didn't know how to do it. He said, "Your sister must be sad you aren't home."

"She not sad," Tusia said.

"I'm sorry."

HORACE SHOWERED AND shaved and put on a fresh white shirt and fresh jockeys and the tan gabardine pants he'd worn yesterday. When Horace left the bathroom, he saw the bed been made and the marble floor had been swept. A boiled egg and a glass of pulpy orange juice waited for him on the gray Formica table. He cracked and salted the egg.

"Thank you, Tusia," he said. Horace said it loud enough for her to hear in the next room, but he was sure she had already gone. The apartment was just too quiet. "Tusia?"

Nothing.

A sudden feeling of emptiness took him. Horace reached into the front pocket of his gabardine pants to touch the gold coin and chain. That was gone, too.

HE HAD RENTED a hospital bed, an electrical one that adjusted to any position, and fixed Celeste a place in the living room. They liked the living room. Their friends could visit. Everybody could talk and watch the plasma TV. During her last days, Celeste was a skeleton with gray skin. She had always been a small woman, five-two, maybe ninety-five pounds on a fat day. Now she looked like a nightmare child.

"If I had my way, I'd live a lot longer," she said. This was her death bed talk. Then Celeste asked the question Horace hated to hear. She said, "What are you going to do after I'm gone?"

"Let's watch the Golden Girls," Horace said and aimed the remote at the TV and clicked.

"You should marry a hot twenty year old," Celeste said and giggled. Her giggle turned into a cough and she reached for the glass of ginger ale that sat within an amber field of medicine bottles on the table next to her. "You know, we should've gone back to Italy," she said. "People don't enjoy themselves enough. Promise me you'll do that. Go back to Italy and enjoy yourself. Think of me, think of us."

"Can I take the twenty year old?" Horace said.

"You're a riot."

After Celeste had died Horace didn't know what to do with himself. He was used to caring for her, cooking meals, doing their laundry, giving her medication, driving her to the hospital for chemo treatments. This was such an uncomplicated way to show his love. Before Celeste got the Big C, she used to do everything, clean the house, cook their meals, wash their clothes, and she liked doing it.

"I'm the laundry and cooking queen," she would say to Horace. "Just call me Your Majesty. Call me little Ms. Susie Homemaker. Ha."

Horace did not understand why she liked all that stuff until the tables were turned and he started doing it. These weren't chores, this wasn't slave labor, it wasn't work or a job. To take care of his Celeste had been his joy. That's how he saw it. There was a sad pleasure in smoothing her days.

"I feel guilty," Celeste would say. This was when her face

was a gray skull and she had no hair. "I used to do and do, and loved it. I did, you know, I loved cooking and doing laundry. Call me crazy. Now you wait on me hand and foot."

"Hey, can't I be Susie Homemaker?" Horace said.

You're a riot." Celeste patted his hand.

"You always watch my back," Horace said. "You take good care of me." He told Celeste this one day while lying next to her on the hospital bed. He had said, "What's good for the gander is good for the goose. Now it's my turn, I deserve that. This isn't a one way street, you know. I deserve to show you my love, too. You shouldn't keep the good times all to yourself."

"I'll miss you," Celeste said. She said it like she and the girls were going to Vegas for the weekend.

"You're my bald-headed sweetie," Horace said and kissed her gray cheek.

The gypsies lived outside the city near Rome's Cinodromo district, an area called Shantytown. Horace had taken the train to Termini in Rome and then a taxi. The driver let him out beside a big muddy field. Horace told him to wait. There were rusted cars and lean-to huts made from scraps of wood and metal. There were patched tents and small graffiti painted trailers. Laundry hung off these homes like Christmas ornaments. Everything looked balanced against everything else.

A fat naked girl with a dirty face was squatting in a tub of water. The old woman in front of the child rested on the steps of her trailer, smoking a cigarette and directing the fat girl's bath. Barefoot children ran between the huts, tents, and trailers. The camp smelled of earth and frying meats, tobacco smoke and urine. Three men were sitting in a circle on wooden chairs. They had muddy feet and wore summer T-shirts and rolled up pants. They smoked cigarettes and talked and gestured to each other. One man laughed; he had no upper teeth.

Horace had his hand cupped above his eyebrows, scanning the camp. There must have been eight hundred to a thousand of these huts, tents, and trailers. The army had sent Horace to Korea in '64, Tague, Pusan, Seoul. He was an AFKN D.J. then, playing Motown and the Stones. Even the bigger cities had muddy streets and huts made from scraps of metal and wood. He saw them when he was riding the trains. Some people who lived in the huts died of asphyxiation in the winter and encephalitis in the summer. Korea was different now, his old friends told him this in their e-mails and letters. What would his friends think of Shantytown? What would they say about the huts, tents, and trailers sprawled along the edge of such a rich and ancient city?

"Sir come for this?" Tusia said. She was holding the gold coin by its chain. Her dark hair had become tangled again. Bits of mud were dried gray on her narrow face and the shins and calves of her skinny legs. She said, "I wait for Sir. I watch the road. I pretend Sir come for me."

Horace knelt, eye-level with her. He felt the cold mud seeping through the knee of his tan gabardines. "I did come to see you," Horace said. "I didn't know it on the train, Tusia, but I know it now. On the train, I wanted my wife's coin back in the worse way. I was so angry. I felt you had stole my wife from me, that tiny part I had left of her."

"Take coin," Tusia said. "I want to see Sir."

"I know," Horace said. He kissed her forehead and placed a white envelope in her hand. Then he said, "I am going back home. You give this to your sister. Or keep it for yourself, buy a gelato. But I'd prefer you buy warm clothes for the winter."

"You take," Tusia said and held up the gold coin.

"Keep it," Horace said. "It was never mine, really. And my wife would've liked the idea."

He slid into the backseat of the cab and heard Tusia calling him after he had shut the door. She was shouting as the cab drove off.

"I go with Sir," she was shouting. "I cook and clean."

American Pastor

THE WINGS WERE never seen but he could hear them. More, really. He could feel and, yes, even smell them. Pastor J.P. Henry will tell you he has felt the feathers touch the rims of his ear, his thin bare arms, his upper legs, the fine blond hair along his neck. There is a burnt chocolate smell to the wings, though not all the time, not every time. The odor changes with mood and circumstance. Pastor Henry will tell you the wings appeared twenty-two years ago after another boy stabbed him in the right ear with the sharp end of a yellow pencil. This was a schoolyard fight at McCook Elementary in Kansas. The wings flap above the young pastor's head and to his right and left, forever out of view. You must turn quickly. No, quicker, quicker! Hurry, look! Doctor Arno, the family G.P., says the wings are an anomaly caused by damage to the ear. J.P. Henry's mother says that is ridiculous, that does not make any sense. "J.P. feels things," Mama Delia says. She also says Pastor J.P. Henry has been blessed with the gift of prophecy and the company of angels.

THERE ARE PEOPLE who will kill you to prove a point. That is what the young pastor thinks. They feed on the words of people they do not know and a fear they cannot name. People will kill you to alter the habits of others. Pastor J.P. Henry knows the fringe element very well. They will love you and hate you far too much.

The fringe. As if this was a decorative thing on a cowboy or the hem of a square dancer's skirt. These afflicted, these emailers and midnight callers who hide in their rooms and watch you on cable TV. How do they get my number? How do you find a person's email address? Pastor J.P. Henry has seen them at the food courts, the discount stores, the concession stands in movie theaters. Their eyes do not match the calmness of their faces.

They will do anything for nothing.

The white Econovan that was at the opposite side of the blacktop is now directly behind Chloe Henry and three year old J.P., Jr. The van's motor idles and the smell of its exhaust mixes with burgers cooking on a grill near the entrance to the grocery store. The Econovan is a newer model, or so the pastor's wife thinks, and the sun glares across the windshield and the polished hood.

Closed windows dull the music coming from a radio or perhaps a CD player. Creedence Clearwater is singing "Born on the Bayou."

Before that there is this. The pastor's wife is pushing a green plastic grocery cart with metal handles and a wobbly left rear wheel across the parking lot of Family Value Foods, seven miles northwest of downtown Wichita. Chloe Henry has skinny legs that have no shape but her face is pretty with what her pastor husband calls "Lovely bone structure." Some men and some women will look at her face a second too long. A July rain has come and gone and the morning sky is clear and hot and the steam from the rain drifts in waves from the blacktop.

The pastor's wife has turned toward the shiny white Econovan, a hand cupped over her brow. Two men are in the front seat and the sun has divided the two men into shadow and light. Chloe Henry cannot see their faces. Then the two men laugh. At a joke? At her? The closed doors and the music do not let the pastor's wife hear the words.

Before that there is this. Twenty or so cars and a clean white Ford Econovan are in the parking lot. A tall man with jeans and a t-shirt and thick pale arms is cooking burgers on a grill near the front entrance to the grocery store. Maybe a

Japanese man, Chloe Henry thinks. No, Chinese. Aren't the Chinese much taller than the Japanese? Brown paper bags fill her plastic shopping cart.

The bags are stuffed with meats and chicken and produce. Each item is wrapped in stretched see through plastic with tough pink Styrofoam bottoms. Other bags hold boxes of breakfast cereal and noodles and thick cylinders of white paper towels. Sitting in a sidekick seat above the brown paper bags is a skinny blond three year old named Justin Perry Henry, Jr. Or J.P., Jr. Or occasionally just Junior. J.P., Jr. has pulled a frosted flakes cereal box from one of the brown bags and his fingertips work to open the top flap. A small blue and red bandage with white stars covers the boy's skinned right knee.

Everything goes way too fast. The man on the passenger's side of the white Econovan is coming toward her. He has thick arms, big teeth and a dead smile. The second man, the man on the driver's side, must be six two or three and he is already opening the back of the van. Music from the radio or CD player rushes through the open doors, another Creedence song. The man coming toward now has on his black sunglasses. His clothes have a burnt cooking oil smell. "I am the angel you have been waiting for," he tells her. The pastor's wife thinks J.P., Jr. would say the man has Bugs Bunny teeth.

Before that there is this. Chloe Henry has stopped the shopping cart at the family's silver SUV and strapped J.P., Jr. into his booster seat. She is busy arranging the brown paper bags in tight rows while ordering Justin Perry, Jr. to please quit messing with the box of frosted flakes. "Give that to mommy," she says and wiggles four slim fingers at the cereal box. "You'll have frosted flakes all over the parking lot," she says. The pastor's wife cannot believe how much she sounds like her own mother.

Long fingers cover Chloe Henry's mouth and nose, a delicate hand. The fingers grip her face but do not hurt her. Wet icy cotton is taped to the smiling man's palm and the wet cotton presses against her nostrils. It reeks of rubbing alcohol or the sweeter smell of gasoline. The man with the dead smile is whispering to Chloe Henry but his words are not precise. His words are static along her skin, the synapses of her brain. His words are electricity popping up from a cheap carpet. The icy feeling goes deep and sharp into her lungs. Chloe Henry cannot steady herself and her legs fold beneath her.

Justin Perry, Jr. has stopped trying to open the sealed top of the frosted flakes. He is now patting the blue and white box with the flat of his small hand and laughing at this new man and his mother. The new man is holding his mother so she won't fall and get hurt. Her skinny arms are loose and dangling in the warm air and her legs that have no shape are bent at funny angles. J.P., Jr. says, "Mommy!" and laughs. Again he slaps the blue and white box with the palm of his hand. When the new man begins dragging his mother to the back of the white Econovan, Justin Perry Jr. is not sure what to do.

"THE LORD WILL lead us and ready us," the pastor's mother had said. "That's what the Lord does best." Pastor J.P. Henry was six years old when Mama Delia drove him to his first revival meeting. Delia had big legs and big hips and wore a shapeless flower print dress that she hoped looked cheerful enough to hide her weight. The white tent was on a piece of farm land off route 81 near Great Bend, the field plowed and darkly wet from an afternoon rain. This was two days after Tucker Davis stuck the sharp end of a yellow pencil through J.P.'s right ear in a schoolyard fight at McCook Elementary. The pain had refused to quit and it was everywhere at once, inside the ear, down his throat, behind his eyes. Even the antibiotic and analgesic prescribed by Doctor Arno did not help.

J.P. and his mother were walking toward the tent under a cloudy spring sky. "You wait, J.P.," his mother had said. "The reverend will lay hands and take your pain. Wait 'til our Lord works His miracle. You can always depend on our Lord." The plowed wet earth sank under the boy's footsteps. Mud lay thick on the toe and heel of J.P.'s dirty white high tops. Delia Henry had an arm about her son and she pressed him to her wide soft hip. Flaps on the big canvas tent snapped and twisted in a warm damp wind. This sounded like a large bird beating its wings. Or that's what J.P. Henry had thought. "Listen to the angels," his mother had said. "Can you hear those angels, J.P.?" The tent had its own noisy life. Wind batted the top and sides. Delia and her boy sat on tan wood fold out chairs under the tall canvas, the roll and the flutter. Delia fed her boy Hershey bars to sooth him. Pastor J.P. Henry remembered the melting chocolate cool on his tongue and the back of his throat. The chocolate tasted and smelled very good and soon he did not think about the pain in his ear.

"Would you like to know what the angels are saying?" his mother whispered. Then she said, You can always count on us. We will follow the Lord and His plan. This was Mama Delia's translation. The wind and the canvas clattered above J.P. Henry. Just show us your good works. You must trust us and show us your good works every day. There are bigger and stronger things than you. Surely you must feel it. Surely you must know it. Delia Henry, interpreter of angels. Mama Delia said these things and fed her boy Hershey bars and waited for the reverend to lay hands.

AN ELDERLY WOMAN named Olive Walker found the pastor's son in the Family Value Foods parking lot with a note duct taped to his chest. The three year old was strapped into the booster seat next to the brown grocery bags. He had a pink arm and a pink leg from sitting close to the rear window in the hot afternoon sun. Mrs. Walker told a KATE TV 4 reporter how J.R., Jr. was in an awful state and had been very tearful. A skinny boy but dressed very well, she said. "You can tell his parents love him." The note taped to the boy's chest was a folded sheet of yellow legal paper. Its five words were cut from magazines and read, You will be contacted, pastor. Mrs. Walker said J.P., Jr. had wet himself and his small narrow face and his white t-shirt were smeared with chocolate and bits of frosted flakes. He'd eaten his way through three Jell-O pudding cups and half a box of cereal.

THE CD DUCT taped to Pastor J.P. Henry's front door is a home movie of his wife and two men. Chloe Henry is tied to a straight back wood chair, her legs and arms like pale sticks, her eyes blindfolded, her mouth gagged. Two men with Lone Ranger masks and black baseball caps stand behind her. This scene reminds Pastor J.P. Henry of the terrorist hostage movies people watch on the cable news shows. The man to the right has a dead smile. A Remington shotgun rests on the crook of a thick arm. His partner is taller and slimmer and is holding the Wichita Eagle newspaper to show the date. Both men wear white dress shirts that are not tucked into their chinos.

The Sedgwick County Sheriff wants Pastor J.P. Henry to identify the two men but the young pastor says the men standing behind his wife do not look familiar. After the movie J.P. Henry asks for directions to the lavatory. The sweat on the pastor's forehead and under his arms is cold from the air conditioning. He cannot stop his body from shaking. The stall door closes behind him and he is on his knees and vomiting into the toilet.

We don't like the job you're doing, pastor. The taller of the two men had said that on the CD home movie. He held the Wichita Eagle next to his face like someone on TV selling peanut butter or a soft drink. And the Lord don't like it, either, let me tell you, the taller man had said. I know that for a fact, sir, a flat out fact. You need to get with the Lord. Here's your problem, sir: you don't listen to the concerns of your fine, well intended parishioners. It's like the logical part of your brain is on a holiday. Taking a cruise to Ghana or Sri Lanka or one of those places you think is so wonderful. Like you're going on your merry way, regardless of good advice. Forget about the folks who foot the bill. See, your problem is this, sir, you have a hard time accepting sincere criticism.

PASTOR J.P. HENRY is resting his forehead on the cool porcelain rim of the toilet bowel. The lavatory of the Sedgwick County Sheriff's Department has the smell of lilac disinfectant and day-old cigarette smoke. Florescent lights hum and pop. These lights are weak and sickly and worse than the dark. Wings have started flapping, softly, softly. Wings flap above J.P. Henry's head and to his right and to his left but away from view. You must turn quickly. No, quicker, quicker! Hurry, look! Feathers stroke the rim of his right ear.

We do not understand you, sir, the taller man said, the man with the Wichita newspaper. Both men stood behind his wife. Blindfolded, gagged, Chloe Henry's skinny legs were bound at the ankles and the knees. 'I do good works,' you say. 'I do the work the Lord has trusted me to do,' you say. But that is the problem, sir, your problem and our dilemma. Your good works are simply not good enough. No, sir, not at all good enough. What about bringing new parishioners to the light? To our Lord? Do you think about their souls, sir? How can a pastor travel to these impoverished place, these filthy little places, and not once mention our Lord?

A florescent light over the lavatory stall has the flicker of a silent movie. On and off, on and off. Pastor J.P. Henry is gripping the porcelain toilet bowel with both hands and praying to God he does not vomit again. What do these two men want from me? the pastor thinks. Actions are louder than words, his mother liked to say. Wings flap to the rhythm of the florescent light, on and off, on and off, wings touch his hair, stroke the rim of his ear, bring him the scent of burnt chocolate.

PASTOR J.P. HENRY has a five state TV congregation. He is syndicated throughout Kansas, Missouri, Oklahoma, Nebraska and Arkansas. He records his service every Sunday morning on KATE TV 4, a small concrete building on West Cessna near the Wichita Mid-Continent Airport. The tiny studio always has two odors, dried grass and bad electrical wiring. The air conditioning is cranked low enough for the young pastor to see his breath. His thin arms and shoulders quiver from the cold. But once the overhead lights heat up he will feel sweat on his neck and the front and back of his shirt and under his arms.

There are viewers who watch Pastor J.P. Henry and write him very long letters and very long emails that ramble and sway to an anger he does not understand. There are phone calls at two or three in the morning, calls that break with courtesy and sensible timing, calls that are too disjointed. Many calls may have jukebox music in the background and talk with no clear words. How do they get my number? Pastor

J.P. Henry thinks. How do they find my email address? Hell is too good for you, they say. May you die slow, you fucker. May you and your family rot in the eternal fire. How can you call yourself an American? they say.

What sort of person tells you that? the young pastor wants to know.

PASTOR J.P. HENRY is driving toward a small gray farm five miles southwest of Colby. One of the two men called and gave him directions. The man also told him the rules that would keep his wife alive. You follow the changes in your sermons, he said. You come by yourself and you come without weapons, he said. You do not speak unless spoken to. Pastor J.P. Henry knew the voice. This was the taller of the two men, the one who held the newspaper in the hostage tape. Yes, definitely the taller man. He has a phlegmy smoker's voice.

Flat green land with leafy soy and new stalks of corn go by the pastor. Dark telephone poles line the sides of the gravel and tar road and the wires glitter in the sunlight. Crows perch on the wires and hide in the rows of corn and soy. Crows shriek at the loud passing trucks and flocks burst from the fields like black reshaping clouds against the blue sky. Exhaust fumes and the odor of earth and straw mix with warm air and rush through the driver's window of the pastor's truck.

There are satellite TV dishes in the front lawns of many farms. The dishes are attached to metal stems and rise up like large black flowers. Pastor J.P. Henry imagines the families in these farms watching his service earlier this morning on their satellite TVs. Just thinking about this embarrasses him. The two men who kidnapped his wife three days ago in the parking lot of Family Value Foods are now ready to release her.

The pastor has done what the two men instructed him to do. J.P. Henry has preached on sin and how to save the soul, the way to heaven and the way to hell. He detailed what the Lord requires to live a devout life.

KATE TV 4 staffers put together the church set late Saturday night, its square patch of red carpet, it's plywood pulpit stained in mahogany with gold painted trim. A velvet curtain hangs behind the pulpit. In front of the curtain and to the right is an American flag on a silver floor stand. A six foot papier-mâché cross sprayed a cherry wood is to the left and suspended with plastic thread. The flag and the papier-mâché cross are new to the church set. Both these items were suggested by the two men who had kidnapped the pastor's wife.

THE FOUR OF them are inside the small gray farm house, the young pastor, his wife and the two men who kidnapped the wife. Sunlight enters through the half raised window and goes over a gray Formica kitchen table and a gray straight back chair in the center of the room. Two blue nylon sleeping bags lie rumpled in a corner. Rope and curled pieces of duct tape are on the gray wood floor and surround the straight back chair. The smell of urine clots the warm air. Along with this is a stale vegetable and fried meat smell.

Chloe Henry has the shotgun that belongs to the man with the thick arms and the dead smile. Her skinny shoulders quiver and her mascara is glittery and wet and blotted about her eyes and streaking her cheeks. She is shouting at the two men who kidnapped her. Pastor J.P. Henry has never heard his wife say such words.

"You disgusting shits," she says. His wife had grabbed the Remington from the Formica table while the man with the thick arms and the dead smile knelt to untie her legs. "Where is my baby, you shits?" she says. Shrieks this, actually. The barrel of the shotgun swerves this way and that. "What have you bastards done with my baby?"

Pastor J.P. Henry tells his wife to relax and listen to him. He says he knows she is angry at the two men and he is also angry at the two men but J.P., Jr. is safe and at home with Mama Delia.

Chloe Henry does not look at her husband. As she pumps out the first shot the young pastor steps between her and the two men. His open hands extend to his wife, waving her down. The shotgun is very loud and Pastor J.P. Henry hears the crows scream outside the window. The pastor hears them leaving the field, the new stalks of corn and the soy. He cannot see the crows. You must turn quickly. No, quicker, quicker! Hurry, look! But he can hear their wings.

THE BUSH STREET WHORES

I HAD WANTED Bunny T.'s hands to turn bony and have thick veins. How wonderful to see his hands that way. Brown spots should linger above paper skin and speckle those sweet elderly hands. I imagined him clutching a metal walker as one tiny step followed the next. His combed back black hair was patchy and white in my daydreams. Many wrinkles cut into his once smooth beautiful face. In my daydreams his clothes were outdated and the years had compromised his elegance. I think my life would have been different if my father had become an old man.

THE DOWNTOWN WHORES would gather at the bars along Bush Street every afternoon at three or four. This was Norfolk before the dinosaurs, mother liked saying. She was a slender woman with frizzed red hair and green-green eyes. My father sold military uniforms and work clothes on Bush Street for Virginia Undersellers from 1943 to the mid-fifties and he knew all the whores by name. Many bars lined the street and there was a permanent pizza and beer smell.

The whores were young and very fat. They wore plastic hair curlers and crayon colored dresses that fit tight. They smoked Chesterfields or Luckies, some smoked king-sized Kools. The whores liked my father and me and liked waving to us and joking around.

"You're going to break some hearts, Curtis," they used to say to me. "See you in a couple of years, hon, they used to say, and laughed. My father laughed with them and rubbed my hair with his long thin fingers."

"What are whores?" I once asked my father this on a Sunday afternoon at City Park. We were feeding the ducks a stale loaf of rye bread. Every duck in the pond was begging for rye.

"Whores stop a man from feeling alone and sorry for himself," my father said. "Some men will never have a woman like your mom."

That afternoon my father talked about the whores and told the ducks there would be enough rye to go around. I don't know why one conversation will haunt you and other conversations will disappear forever.

Mother thought I was a miniature version of my father. She called him Bunny T. but his name was Burgess Thomas Hickey. One of our photographs showed Bunny T. tossing a baseball while dressed in a gray three piece pinstriped and starched white shirt. My father dressed to the minute and smelled of eucalyptus cologne. He was tall but not too skinny, and he had combed back black hair and a face with smooth edges. Mother said Bunny T.'s face was so beautiful it could make friends without him.

Curtis Hickey has been thinking about his years in Tacoma and Korea while waiting at Norfolk International for his fiancée's three-ten flight from O'Hare. He is sitting in an orange plastic seat on a front row of other orange plastic seats. His long legs extend straight to the floor and cross at the ankles. He was his dad's boy, that's what his mother would say. Bunny T. had the looks, let me tell you, his mother would say. Curtis Hickey is wearing tan chinos and loafers with no socks. The row of orange seats are close to the large observational window and overlook the airplanes working the runways. Metal wings and tails send sunlight through the window and onto the white walls and the dull worn carpet. A nearby magazine and food stand has an odor of popcorn and grilling hot dogs.

The young woman who became Curtis Hickey's fiancée had given him the sleeve to her favorite yellow Oxford shirt. Curtis met her while he was in the Army. She was the daughter of his battalion commander.

"You should take this to Korea," Patty Ann said and handed him a slim box with the sleeve in it. "Knights are supposed to carry the woman's scarf into battle," she said. Patty Ann looked everywhere but at Curtis Hickey. She was a small girl with ear-length blond hair and very pale skin. Her face had angular cheekbones and a small sculpted nose. The skin was pocked on the chin and forehead by oil and hormones. Her yellow sleeve was hemmed at the shoulder to keep it from threading. "I don't have an actual scarf," Patty Ann said.

Curtis Hickey did not think he was a knight. The United States Army had promised him a college education for three years service. So he became a disc jockey at the American Forces Korean Network in Seoul. The yellow sleeve had been starched and ironed and its white plastic button hooked into the cuff. Patty Ann's sleeve was sprayed with a young girl's perfume. It had been sprayed more than once, that's what Curtis Hickey had thought. The scent reminded him of sugar cookies. Patty Ann's perfume let him imagine a better, safer place. Curtis Hickey would breathe in her perfume and see Patty Ann parking her father's new sixty-two Dodge Dart just off the main parade ground at Fort Lewis. The Tacoma night was cold and snowy, and the snow hid the moon and covered the car windows. Warm breath had fogged the glass inside the Dodge Dart. Curtis Hickey did not think Patty Ann was his lover but he had unbuttoned her yellow Oxford shirt and kissed her breasts and knew that counted for something.

MY FATHER DIED from a heart attack at age forty-two with the Bush Street whores and me shaking our Bunny T. and trying to help him stay in this world.

He had grabbed the center of his chest with both hands like a cowboy shot in a quick draw and said, "Oh, shit."

That's when he fell to the pavement. My father must have said "oh, shit" three or four times. Bunny T. looked scared, more scared than I thought he could get. A few seconds later he had no expression at all. I could smell my father's piss and his bowel. Bunny T. died at night on the sidewalk in front of Virginia Undersellers. We had worked together that Saturday afternoon. He was locking the store when the heart attack took him. Color and fear left my father's face like bathwater down a drain. The bars along Bush Street were playing their jukeboxes, Little Richard, Hank Williams, Bill Haley and the Comets singing Rock Around the Clock. The whores and me shouted at my father to get up and quit acting funny. I was thirteen and thought men should not show their feelings. But we were crying, the whores and Yours Truly. They said everything would be okay. And if things were not okay they would take care of me. I would have a home, they said. One whore told me she had three babies and one more baby would be fine with her. The idea that I might have both a father and a mother did not occur to them. The bars along Bush Street reflected lights on the pavement. Neon signs were white, pink and blue. Cartoon Tom cats in zoot suits and wide brim hats made huba-huba eyes at female cats who had beehive hairdos and mesh stockings. There were neon silhouettes of naked women with finger length nipples. A huge tongue circled a pair of red lips. At night the signs flickered and moved. A few sailors had finished with the bars and had stepped outside to see who could piss across the narrow street or who could piss and hit a passing car.

CLOUDS HAVE MOVED in thick and dark beneath the sunlight and changed the day. There is both thunder and bright shocks of lightening. Rain is blurring the observational window. Rain glistens the planes waiting on the runways at Norfolk International.

Curtis Hickey is still seated in the orange plastic seat in a row of orange plastic seats that face the large window. The yellow sleeve his fiancée gave him before he left for Korea is in the pocket of his chinos. He is rubbing the yellow sleeve with a thumb and forefinger while looking out the window at the rain pelting the airplanes and collecting into shallow pools on the runways.

Curtis Hickey has carried the yellow sleeve for more than two years. He will not go anywhere without Patty Ann's yellow sleeve. He had tied the sleeve about his neck as he boarded the ship to Inchon, Korea. Over three thousand soldiers were on that ship. Most of the soldiers vomited during the night. But Curtis Hickey escaped the stink and the noise. He sat in a passageway below the main deck with an army blanket over his head and his hands pressed to his ears.

The top button to his fatigues was open and he breathed in the sugar cookie perfume Patty Ann had sprayed on the yellow sleeve of her Oxford shirt.

Lightning strikes the runway and brings thunder. Curtis

Hickey has been watching the rain against the observational window and thinking about his new fiancée. She is a nineteen year old journalism major at the University of Kansas in Lawrence who has written him about Schopenhauer and her roommate's allergies and the Warren Commission's flawed report on the Kennedy assassination.

Her last letter before he rotated back to the States was something else entirely.

"Yes, yes, I will marry you," Patty Ann wrote in a tiny precise script. This was the letter Curtis Hickey read two weeks before he left Korea for the States.

"It is night," Patty Ann wrote, "and I am alone in my room now and I am choosing you. I cannot believe what I am doing. But I am choosing you, Curtis. My handsome, beautiful Curtis. Daddy will be a madman, of course. You know Daddy. He cannot understand what a woman might see in an enlisted man," she wrote. "But Daddy is not marrying you, is he? I am marrying you. I am marrying you, I am marrying you. (I love writing that. Ha ha.) Daddy will just have to get used to the idea. We have to live our own lives, don't we? We decide what is right for us. Our lives are our responsibility. Isn't that right, Curtis? I can picture you nodding your head and smiling your amazing smile, I really can. Mommy says you should always consider the man who cheers you on."

I STAYED INSIDE the limousine, that I remember very well.

The rear windows were tinted and the sunny morning had a sepia color. People wore black suits and dresses and the women wore black hats with laced veils. Four of the Bush Street whores drove up in an old brown Ford that had a rusted fender and a red ping pong ball on the radio antenna. The whores parked next to the gravesite behind our limousine. They also stayed in the car but waved to me and blew kisses. Bunny T. was buried beside my mother's mother. Sunlight showed between the oaks and the pines and the rows of boxwood. Even with the limousine window rolled shut I could smell the boxwood. Sunlight reflected on my father's mahogany casket and the brass poles that held the casket over his open grave.

"THERE IS AN extra plot for you," Mother had said on the way to the cemetery. Her voice was quiet and shaky. She wore a shiny black straw hat with a black veil. We were sitting in the limo on the leather backseat. Shadows surrounded mother but I could see her red lipstick under the veil. She had a lilac perfume that was too strong and padded the air. "There is a plot for me next to Bunny," my mother said. "And one for you next to me."

I was thirteen years old with fantasies that did not ask my permission for anything. I had imagined myself as an orphan and living in a one room shack that had no heat or central air. I imagined my mother nesting next to Bunny T. in their separate buffed coffins like two renters in a mahogany and brass duplex. More, really. I imagined my parents doing

robbed and raped all the time, thrown into the back of mini vans, left on the side of the road. Poor Judy Ray, poor Jessica, poor what's her name. Hasn't he seen the victim's parents and friends on the TV news? She was always doing volunteer work, they would say. A darling, friendly girl who loved helping others, they would say. Curtis Hickey used to have the same thoughts in Korea if Patty Ann missed a day writing to him. He is remembering his fiancée's letters while looking out the large observational window at Norfolk International, the slanted rain, the planes lifting off and landing. An odor of popcorn and grilling hot dogs from the nearby magazine and food stand has Curtis Hickey checking the money in his black leather wallet.

"I am going out with a lieutenant," Patty Ann had written this to Curtis Hickey in a much earlier letter. "His name is Griffin and he is a West Point graduate."

This was during his fiancée's back and forth period. She had dated the lieutenant for three months. And for three months Curtis Hickey slept an hour or two a night and ate an occasional peanut butter and jelly sandwich. In his letters he pleaded with Patty Ann to marry him and felt puzzled and ashamed by his behavior. When Curtis Hickey did sleep he dreamed of dark empty fields that went on forever. He would feel hot panic soak into him.

"You can just imagine how thrilled Daddy is," Patty Ann wrote. "A West Point man, Daddy is beside himself. You would think I was dating Jesus."

Curtis Hickey has settled himself into the orange plastic seat in front of the observational window. The sky goes bright with lightning and there is muted thunder.

"What are we supposed to do, exactly?" Isn't that what the young flight attendant told him? "We are at the mercy of the elements," she had said.

The rain stopped earlier but the streets are slick and reflect the lights from the buildings and the traffic. Curtis Hickey is now driving down City Hall Avenue toward Bush Street. There are banks and tall narrow buildings of tinted glass and tan and rust colored bricks. An evening sky is threaded purple and pink. He walked out on his fiancée after she had excused herself to use the lavatory.

"Point me to the little girl's room," Patty Ann said. Then she said, "A girl has to pay her water bill."

Who was this woman he wanted so badly?

His fiancée had dropped her green leather suitcase and run to him. High heels wobbled on the worn carpet. She wore a tight gray dress with printed pink flowers. Patty Ann's neck and thighs were thicker than he remembered. Damp half circles showed beneath fleshy arms. Her hair was pulled back into a ragged French twist, hair more brown than blond. Curtis Hickey had not liked the kiss. Patty Ann's embrace was abrupt, more an assault than an embrace. Her right arm hooked his neck and yanked him to her mouth. The lips were dry and rough, her breath smelled of cigarettes and over-cooked vegetables. Who is this woman? he had thought. What does she want with me? His Patty Ann lived in the back seat of her daddy's Dodge Dart with the evening snow whirling around. His Patty Ann was small and blond and sometimes her shoulders would quiver when he touched her.

Who was this woman at the airport?

THE YELLOW SLEEVE is curled flat on the passenger's seat. Its frayed eyehole will not stay hooked to the plastic button. Fingertips and traveling have soiled the material. Before Curtis Hickey climbed into his car at the airport he had inhaled his fiancée's yellow sleeve like it was oxygen but he could not smell her sugar cookie perfume. He had felt light headed and pressed both hands on the hood of the car to keep his balance. It never occurred to him that Patty Ann's perfume would not be there.

Virginia Undersellers is gone. Curtis Hickey has parked in front of what was once his father's store but is now a crimson brick building with two big ATM machines on either sides of double glass doors. The ATM machines glow like phosphorous green eyes. Bush Street is part of Norfolk's new financial district, very upscale, very la-de-da. Curtis Hickey used to drive this street with his father, three maybe four years ago. They always had good talks. Bunny T. liked to laugh and rub Curtis Hickey's hair with his long slim hand. Bunny T. would try to answer all his son's questions, even the ones about the Bush Street whores with their big plastic curlers and crayon colored dresses.

"Whores stop a man from feeling alone and sorry for himself," his father had said.

The salt and fish of the Elizabeth River have replaced the stale pizza and beer smell Curtis Hickey knew as a child. There are no more bars with neon Tom cats giving the eye to kitties in black mesh stockings. No more neon women lure you with finger length nipples. Gone is the flicker and the jump of electric signs. Gone are the sailors who would step outside the bars to piss across the narrow street. Wood benches are beside the new brick and glass buildings. Young oaks and maples have been planted by the curbs.

Curtis Hickey's head is leaning against the cloth backrest of the car. He has shut his eyes. His hands and legs begin to shake and he does not know what to do about it.

"The whores were young and very fat," Curtis Hickey says out loud.

He imagines Bunny T. sitting beside him in a gray three piece pinstripe and a starched white shirt.

"They smoked Chesterfields or Luckies," Curtis Hickey says. "Some smoked king-sized Kools," he says.

He remembers the whores waving and laughing. Bunny T. was laughing, too. Curtis Hickey is waiting for his father's long thin fingers to touch his hair.

Dangerous Boy

He did not resemble the man who married his mother. Willis Rodel was thin with blond hair that would not stay combed. The man who married his mother had black hair that he brushed again and again until the hair obeyed him. People would breathe in the man's peppery cologne before they knocked on the front door. For Willis Rodel's ninth birthday his mother bought him a dozen books by Edgar Rice Burrows. The man hid the books and said nothing. The man who married his mother had given Willis Rodel his last name but not his square weighty body or the big thick hands that could grab you and shake you and not let you go.

His Japanese neighbor walked up behind Willis Rodel as he cocked his rusted golf club to hit a croquet ball across the front yard. Rain had gone through Norfolk during the night and the morning was hot and the grass was still wet and Talbert Park had a breakfast, maple syrup smell. Sunlight showed steam rising from the lawns. His Japanese neighbor was Momoko Enoki. She had a roundtan face with tiny perfect teeth and smooth eyelids. Momoko was ten and a girl of extremes. She liked to run up and down her porch steps. She yelled and laughed and ordered invisible people to do this and that in Japanese. Momoko also liked being with Willis Rodel on the roof of a vacant cinder block shed at the end of their street. This was where the street stopped and became a marshland. Tan grass and trees with crooked black trunks grew in the streams and the gray mud. A sulfur odor that smelled like rotted eggs traveled the breeze. Momoko and Willis Rodel would lie on their backs and feel the sun or the damp air, whatever the day brought them. That's when Willis Rodel told Momoko his stories. The stories always had an old mansion with many rooms and each room had something scary inside the closet or under the bed or in the corner. There were spiders and dead people who smelled bad and a hand without its body. You could find poisonous jewelry and a fat man who had no bones and sharp black teeth. Willis Rodel loved telling Momoko stories. She would squeal and giggle and hold tight to his arm.

Willis Rodel hit his neighbor below her left eye with his golf club but he did not do it on purpose. Sunshine was glittering the morning. Silver and gold flashes came from the wet grass and the trees and the pruned shrubs by the house. Willis Rodel had cocked his rusted golf club to hit the croquet ball and heard a collision of club and bone. Momoko collapsed and covered her round tan face with both hands.

"Ohhh," she said. She said it the way you do when air is snatched from your lungs.

Blood seeped between stubby fingers and bits of cut grass stuck to her knees. Bright orange shoelaces dangled from Momoko's scuffed high tops.

Willis Rodel did not know what to do. She's dead, he had thought. I murdered Momoko. Oh Jesus. His body felt cold and hot at the same time. The feelings were strong enough to bring sweat and a tremor to his shoulders and his skinny legs.

Momoko Enoki began screaming but her hands did not leave her face. Blood oozed about her fingers and onto her wrists and down her tan arms.

"Oh Jesus," Willis Rodel said.

HUGH RODEL WAS the name of the man who married Willis's mother. Hugh had small pale scars on his jaw and chin from high school wrestling and a beard he could never shave away completely. Hugh shuttled corporate people to Philadelphia, New York and Boston in his helicopter. The man who married his mother enjoyed reading the morning newspaper in a forest green chair by the living room window. Sun sparkled the dust about the Venetian blinds and the dust turned to gold. Hugh would stretch his legs and trip Willis Rodel as the boy ran to the front door and the waiting school bus. Books and a metal lunch box flew into the white sunshine and the dust and over the gray carpet. The man who married Willis Rodel's mother did not lower his paper. He was a voice concealed by the news of the day.

"Not very quick on your feet, huh, boy?" That's what Hugh had said.

The marriage lasted close to a year. Then Hugh drove off to get his Navy blue Italian wool from the cleaners and kept on driving.

"YOU DID WHAT?" Now his mother hit Willis Rodel's bedroom door with the fleshy side of her fist. "Unlock this damn thing," Eunice said.

Her eyes were large and dark and nervous. She was bony and small like her son. Her skin would burn in the summer but did not tan. Eunice wore pink sandals with clear plastic heels and new jeans that were frayed at the knees when she had bought them. Her hair was tangled and thready and blond.

"I am going to count to three," Eunice said. "Okay? Okay? I am going to count to three and march outside and grab the first man I see and tell him to beat down this door. You got it mister? Am I clear?"

"I hit the Japanese girl in the eye with my golf club," Willis Rodel said this from the other side of the door.

The golf club belonged to the man who had married his mother. Willis lay in the bed and looked at the shadowed ceiling. The veins in his neck ached from a heart beating too fast and too hard. He imagined himself being executed for killing the Japanese girl. An electric current fried his insides until smoke poured from his mouth. Needles shot poison into his thin arms and his legs. Thick bristled rope cracked his neck as he fell into the darkness.

"I didn't kill Momoko on purpose," Willis Rodel said to the closed bedroom door. "People have accidents," he said in a whisper. He felt his stomach go tight and start to cramp. "You're supposed to be my mother," he said. "Don't people have accidents?"

"You hate it when I am happy," his mother said and slapped at the bedroom door with the flat of her hand. "Hugh told me this would happen," she said. "The man is a prophet. He has a gift, Willis, he has these genuine tendencies. You underestimated the man. Hugh once told me, 'You watch that Willis. You got yourself one dangerous boy. Oh I know he is your son and all and you love him, Eunice. But love is truly blind,' that's what Hugh said. He said, 'You got a boy who hates thinking you could be happy with someone besides him.' The man was a true prophet."

Willis Rodel was about to say he did not kill Momoko Enoki to make his mother unhappy but he heard the front door open and slam shut and knew he was alone.

Two older kids on muddy trail bikes hopped the curb and weaved through the white crape myrtles and the rows of boxwood. They were hunched over silver handlebars and racing toward Willis Rodel who was looking at his next door neighbor's blood and waiting for a police car to park itself in his driveway. There were nine dried crimson drops the size of quarters on the Japanese girl's concrete and brick porch. A few drops were dulled by shadows. Willis Rodel's mother had driven Momoko Enoki and Mrs. Enoki to the emergency room at Norfolk General. Eunice had left her son a note pinned to the screen door. Crape myrtles and boxwood were wet from last night's rain and glistened under a morning sky that had no clouds. The older boy on the trail bike could have been a sixth or a seventh grader. He had black rimmed sunglasses and a Baltimore Orioles baseball cap. The other boy was probably a fifth grader and closer to Willis Rodel's age. This younger one had slender white arms and his sunglasses were mirrors and hid his eyes. The two boys stopped their bikes at the steps of the Japanese girl's porch.

"Me and Wayne saw you hit that girl," the older one said to Willis Rodel. Both trail bikes had a rotted eggs odor from the marshland at the end of the street. Gray mud was dripping from their tires onto the sunlit pavement. The boy with the slender arms and the mirrored sunglasses grinned. He had a space between his front teeth.

"You tried to kill that fat Jap girl," the younger boy said. "I mean you really wanted to knock her brains out."

Then the one with the black rimmed sunglasses and the Orioles baseball cap said, "I can tell your future. My grandma taught me," he said. The boy was straddling his trail bike. He lifted the bike by the handlebars and bounced the tires to shake off the gray wet mud. "Go stand behind the blood," the older boy said. "I can see an aura if you stand behind the blood."

The younger one who had the slender arms and the mirrored sunglasses was nodding and looking serious. He also started bouncing his tires on the pavement.

"G.W. has a talent," the younger boy said and glanced at the older boy but did not smile at him or change his serious look. "G.W. can tell you some unbelievable shit," the younger boy said.

Willis Rodel was not sure if he wanted the older boy to tell him the future. Some unbelievable shit needed to stay a secret, that's what Willis Rodel thought. The blood spots on the concrete and brick porch had dried now and looked more like brown paint than blood.

The older boy adjusted his baseball cap so the brim touched his black sunglasses and shaded his face. "What can I say?" the older boy said. "My grandma gave me the gift. That's what she called it, the gift. And her mama gave it to her. My grandma could tell you stuff you don't want to know. So how about it?" the older boy said." I can tell you if the fat Jap girl is going to die or whatever. I can tell you if you're going to the penitentiary."

WILLIS RODEL HAD cut the man who married his mother with a kitchen knife. He had cut Hugh on the top of his big right arm, a good cross cut, a three or four incher. Blood flowed from the cut and matted the black hair on the man's arm. "You little asshole. You fuck," that was what the man who married his mother had said. "Can't you take a joke?

What sort of a kid can't take a joke?" he said.

Hugh Rodel's color had gone from his face and his mouth was open and his dark eyes blinked like Morse code. He watched the blood leave his big arm and change the porcelain kitchen sink to red. The man was letting cold water clean the cut. Blood turned pale and swirled into the drain.

"That hurts like a bitch," the man said but his eyes had no expression. There was a bacon and toast smell in the kitchen and the bacon and toast smell mixed with the man's peppery cologne.

"You aren't my father," Willis Rodel said. "You don't ever punch me, you hear? You do not do that. You got no right to punch somebody else's kid," the boy said.

Close to ten minutes ago the man who married his mother had struck Willis Rodel in the stomach for going into the refrigerator and drinking the man's orange juice.

"I hope you're happy," Hugh said. "This hurts like a bitch. Why can't you take a joke? he said. Why are you such a head case?" The man was watching the blood and the cold water roll from his thick hairy forearm. "I was just playing with you," Hugh said. "You should thank Jesus you got me. Some kids don't have shit." The man who had married Willis Rodel's mother was now pressing a blue and white striped hand towel against the cut on his right forearm and saying, "You're lucky to have me. You're lucky to have my name." The man peeked under the towel as he talked. "You don't have a goddamn soul but me and your mom," he said.

The boy had once asked his mother to tell him about his real father.

"He left before you were born," Eunice said but she had looked at the gray living room carpet when she had said it. "Your daddy didn't want a child," Eunice said. "It never occurred to me that the man I loved would not want children. Who knew such a thing? I was too protected growing up, too naïve. But men can be like that," she said. "Men can love you and get stubborn and throw it away. Your daddy was a good man but he wasn't father material. He was not a mature man." Willis Rodel thought about his mother and his real father. He held the kitchen knife and watched the man who was not his father peek under the blue and white striped towel.

"You do not touch me," Willis Rodel said. He was ready to cut the man again if he tried anything. "You don't hit somebody else's kid in the stomach," he said.

"WHAT ARE YOU supposed to see?" Willis Rodel said this to the older boy on the bicycle and wanted to know how much longer he needed to stand behind thedried blood Momoko had left on her concrete and brick porch. Willis had no idea if the older boy in the Orioles baseball cap could tell the future. He wasn't sure if people could tell you the future and he knew nothing about this kid. The older boy and his friend went to his school but they never spoke to him. The one who looked close to Willie Rodel's age was not in any of his classes.

They stayed to themselves, these two boys, these little

criminals. That's what the man who had married his mother would have called them, "these little criminals." The two boys only liked each other. They watched the girls before classes and they ate lunch together. After school the two boys stood in front of the deli shop on the corner and smoked Pall malls, or the big shot sixth grader did. The older boy's grandmother might have given him the gift. That might be true, some old folks talked like they could see your future.

"Nobody's going to put me in a penitentiary," Willis Rodel said. "I'm a kid. I mean I won't be ten until August. You don't put a nine year old in a penitentiary," he said and looked down at his skinny legs and flicked off the wet grass from his shins and knees with a thumb and forefinger.

He did not know if there were kids in the penitentiary. Willis Rodel could smell rotted egg, the gray mud from the marshland. Both boys had the mud on their trail bikes. Willis felt his stomach go tight. A sick feeling came to the back of his throat.

"I thought you had the gift," Willis Rodel said to the older boy.

"Oh I got the gift", the older boy said. "They got a penitentiary for kids, too," he said.

"It's got bars like a real penitentiary," younger one with the mirrored sunglasses said. His legs straddled his muddy trail bike. Slender white arms were folded one on the other and rested chest level against his green short sleeve polo shirt. "They got guards with guns and everything," he said.

"This don't seem good for you," the older boy said to

Willis Rodel. He was looking at the dried quarter sized drops of blood on Momoko Enoki's concrete and brick porch. "A healthy aura has lots of color," he said. "What you got is a gray fog. It's almost black."

"Uh-oh," the younger boy said.

"Don't look good," the older one said.

WILLIS RODEL HAD fallen asleep on the roof of the abandoned cinder block shed at the end of the street, that in between place where the marshland began.

The rotted egg, sulfur odor was very strong and the sun had turned orange now.

Light went about the black branches and the tall brown grass and laid shade on the ground. The air did not have the heat of the morning. Clouds were long and thready in the blue sky. The tar and asbestos roof left Willie Rodel feeling heavyand tired. His shoulders ached.

He imagined his mother had already called the police.

"You got to come and get my dangerous boy," that was what he imagined his mother saying. "Hugh warned me," she would tell the police. "The man is a prophet. He has these genuine tendencies." Willis Rodel imagined his suitcase packed and next to the front door.

"Nobody knows I am here," Momoko Enoki said. She was standing under an oak tree near the cider block shed and looking up at him.

Bright orange shoestrings were untied and dangled from

her high tops. The shadows of the leaves fluttered over her. A bandage covered Momoko's left eye and part of her cheek. She wore the clothes she had on that morning but there were dried spots of blood on the t-shirt and khaki shorts.

"Your mom came over our house looking for you," Momoko said. "Your mom is very emotional."

"I thought you were dead," Willis Rodel said.

"Me too," she told him. "I thought you had knocked my head off.

Momoko asked Willis Rodel if he would come down from the roof now and walk her home.

Orange sunlight outlined and sparkled the leaves and the branches of the trees along both sides of the street. The trees were wide and heavy on top and the tops leaned toward one another and made a shady archway. A breeze from the marshland brought the smell of sulfur and damp grass. Momoko held onto Willis Rodel's right arm. He felt her tan fingers pressing into his skin.

"Will you tell me about the big house with all the rooms?" Momoko said. "Talk about the rooms, please," she said. "Tell me what's scary in the closet and under the bed."

Considering Her In Harry's Bar

THE YOUNG SOLDIER has traveled 3,200 miles to hurt her, not that he wants to, not that he doesn't love her. He will say, "I'm married. I got married in the desert. And the woman isn't even American or Italian, she's a Baghdad girl."

People go to Venice during the winter for Carnevale. Most men dress in black capes and tricon hats and white masks that have no expression. The soldier wears his class A greens and beret, but the medals are in his pocket. They make him feel uncomfortable. He must rest his weight on a brown lacquered cane with a silver handle.

Both the Grand Canal and the late morning have a rough winter look. His water taxi bounces and slaps the lagoon's cold green surface. Then steel cranes emerge through the fog, followed by scaffolding, the tools of repair. Venice must constantly glue herself together. When the Basilica and the Palazzo Ducale come into view, the soldier stiffens his back and cups a hand to his brow. The Grand Canal has swollen an inch or two over the docks. Wood planks crisscross Piazza San Marco.

The owner of Harry's Bar remembers him from two years ago. Last summer Mr. Marcari turned seventy-two. He's the son of the original owner, and his talent for putting a name with a face surpasses his father.

"Vincent," he says and momentarily embraces the boy. "The padrone's table, that's you, si? You always request the writer's table. And the double martini, you order the double martini like him. I don't forget."

Marcari is short, five-three or four, thinning white hair cropped close. A gray gabardine, starched white shirt, and mauve tie give an elegant but fastidious appearance. The old man's smile folds abruptly into itself. He has noticed the lacquered cane and the young soldier's leg.

As they walk toward the table at the far wall, Marcari says, "How's your beautiful Rebecca?"

"She's the reason I'm here," Vincent says. He allows the old man to help him with the chair.

His parents wanted him in Venice. This was in the fall of 2002. U.S. and British forces had already conducted six air strikes on Iraqi targets.

"You need to leave the country," his mother says. "I want you alive. Is that too much to ask? You're my only child, my sweet boy, and I won't have crazy people taking you from me."

They live in New York, an east village brownstone. His mother is a novelist who has used many pseudonyms and typically writes romances and mysteries; his father, a tenured professor of Middle Eastern Studies at N.Y.U. They are card carrying members of what is now called "the blue states." His father calls them, "the states that think." His father also says, "This is still a cowboy war. Children are going to get themselves crippled or killed."

Mr. Marcari brings the double martini. It's served in a small round glass with no olive and tastes the same as a double shot of cold vodka. The room has less than a dozen dark wood tables. At dinner they are cloaked in yellow linen, but it's five-fifteen, three hours too early for the drinking and dining crowd. Except for an older woman by the bar sipping a Bellini, Harry's is empty.

Vincent invites the old man to sit, saying: "I'm supposed to meet Rebecca near the Basilica at eight. Another dumb idea of mine." Vincent looks into the martini and tells the old man about his recent marriage to the Baghdad girl. He says, "I thought talking face to face with Rebecca was best, now I don't know. I should've written a letter. We were good at that. When I was away, we wrote all the time."

Vincent stayed in a Venetian neighborhood called San Marcuola for the winter of 2002 and through the summer of 2003. He cooked and waited tables for a kosher bar and restaurant named Gam-Gam. This is where he met Rebecca who was studying fashion design at the Accademica Italiana in Rome. Her thick black hair was kept loosely tied with a string of turquoise beads. Her eyes had a silvery blue tint. Rebecca's beauty unsettled Vincent. He wondered why she had picked him. He wondered when she would regret her choice.

They lived together for three months before Vincent decided to return home and join the Army. Of course his mother pleaded with him to reconsider. These talks always ended badly, the mother sobbing, the son giving comfort. Between her tearful sessions were his father's rational monologues that posed the question: "What reasons can you give me for such a decision?" Vincent wasn't sure. He felt better joining the Army than not joining it.

A sip of the icy martini leaves a burn in the back of his throat. Mr. Marcari watches the boy then says: "I once met a friend of the writer's. Our writer who used to sit at this table. The friends was a military man, a general. Very big deal, the general. Perhaps not as big a deal as our padrone but he was important in his own way." Marcari stops to flick something invisible from the sleeve of his gray gabardine. He says, "When these two big deals would get together, all the general wanted to talk about was his own writing. To ask the advice of the padrone. Yet all our writer wanted to talk about was courage. The general couldn't believe the man's obsession. 'Courage crap', the general called it."

Vincent takes a second sip of the vodka martini. The burn is less now. He feels the tension in his shoulders begin to subside. "That's why I like his books," Vincent says. "The bulls in Pamplona, that man against nature stuff, the war. But I never considered what any of it meant 'til I was driving through

Baghdad. You look at those poor bastards in the streets and try to guess who's going to leap into your Humvee and blow his ass up. And my ass along with him. When you're talking about courage over there, you're just figuring out how to get through the day."

Vincent's bride is Nisreen Mohammed Jassim Al-Naseri. The first name is her own; the second, her father's; the third, her grandfather's. The last one is the name of her tribe. Nisreen was an interpreter assigned to his unit, the 4th Infantry, which arrived in Iraq right after the fall of Baghdad.

During his team's nightly house to house search for insurgents, she went along to translate. Vincent would greet the local who answered the door, Nisreen right there with him. "Masaa' innoor," she'd say. But situations can go wrong quickly. An insurgent with an AK-47 had hidden beneath a blanket, pretending to sleep. The rife barrel appeared and swept toward Nisreen. Vincent fired twice, both shots hitting the man's chest. That was his first and last up close kill. Nisreen's only comment had been, "A woman in my position insults them." After killing the insurgent, Vincent stopped being polite. He couldn't kill and be considerate at the same time.

Nisreen started visiting him during lunch, while he was standing guard. She brought sandwiches and talked about whatever came to mind. It's not easy starting a romance in the Baghdad sun. Temperatures can reach a hundred and thirteen easy. A hundred and a quarter isn't out of the question. Sand storms can cut you. It can slice a cornea, fill the throat. War is a relative thing.

The woman has her own beauty, though perhaps not as lovely as Rebecca. Dark hair, dark eyes, her body is husky, more bulk to the thighs and arms. Nisreen presented herself as self-contained rather than delicate, a protector instead of someone who needed protecting. That appealed to Vincent, particularly living in a place like Baghdad where everything seemed to require his vigilance.

Nisreen was the first to mention marriage. Born in Iraq, she'd moved to America at the age of five and had dual citizenship. "Iraqi men marry whoever they want," she said. "Iraqi women can only marry Muslims. But an American woman, she chooses her marriage." Then Nisreen touched Vincent's cheek with her palm and said, "Our Muslim men, they're incensed by American women. You think you're fighting terrorists? Is that what you think? This is a religious war, Vincent. It's been going on for centuries. This war is a quarrel over morals, a fight about how the world should act."

At 7:20 PM, Harry's Bar has on its evening clothes, its yellow linen table cloths, its folded napkins and silverware. The second double martini doesn't burn at all. Vincent leans back in his chair and he listens to Mr. Marcari talk about the writer.

"I loved the man, he was like family," Marcari is telling him. "I remember, one evening he confessed to me. He said, 'Arrigo, I write about love and war. And I've failed miserably at both.' Of course, I try to reassure the padrone that wasn't the case, but he waved me off. He said, 'Why do you think I write so well about them?'" Marcari shrugs, gazes down at his manicured fingernails. "I'm an old man now," he says. "I can tell you he was right. He had bad luck with the women, and couldn't hunt. The padrone would drive to Caorle for the duck hunt in his black limousine. All the hunters, they shoot fifty, sixty ducks. The padrone, four." Marcari hold up four fingers and grins. "True story." His teeth are too even and too white.

Vincent glances at his watch. He imagines Rebecca waiting on the wood boards that crisscross a flooded Piazza San Marco. He wonders if she still wears the turquoise beads to hold her hair.

Marcari studies the young soldier's face. He says, "You worry about the girl?" Vincent sips his martini, the vodka cold and smooth as it slides down his throat. "Yes, I worry," Vincent says "I worry that I'll hurt her. I worry that she won't care enough to be hurt."

The old man nods, something of a wistful look coming to him. "Young women love a man with a cane," Marcari says. "The padrone also had a leg injury during the war. While driving his ambulance. He was shipped to a Milan hospital and promptly fell in love with his nurse."

Vincent's team had been doing a daylight door to door search along the periphery of Baghdad, the more rural areas, when a freak downburst storm took them. Wind rushed vertically to the ground at 60 to 80 M.P.H., thrusting out a 3,000 foot high wall of sand and dust. It first turned the sky deep orange then black, more a ground level tornado than a typical sandstorm, all of this happening in under a minute. Two of the team were swept into the gritty air and thrown fifteen, maybe twenty yards. Vincent heard the blast right away. Ten million land mines are buried in Iraq. The one that killed the two men on his team was a Valmara 69. Stepped on, the Valmara 69 propels upward and detonates at waist level, obliterating the lower part of the body. Vincent grabbed Nisreen and dove into a roadside gully thick with brush, his body atop her, back to the explosion. The whistling of the shrapnel was everywhere. A second or two later he felt the metal cut and burn his hip, his thigh, along the length of his leg.

Mr. Marcari is signaling to Claudio to seat a newly arrived couple at the corner left table. The drinking and dining crowd is now steadily filling Harry's Bar.

"I must leave you, Vincent," Marcari says. He fidgets with the cuffs of his white shirt then, as an afterthought, he says, "The general and our writer friend were very different men. I the loved the padrone like a boy loves the black sheep uncle. The difference between them is this, the black sheep uncle, he shoots himself. But when the general dies, they bury him at Arlington." Marcari stands, brushes the wrinkles from his gray gabardine. He tells the young soldier, "That general, he says to me once, 'Courage isn't what a sober person discusses in public.' Then Marcari says, "You'll find your words, Vincent."

The night has cleared the fog. Narrow wet streets reflect

the moonlight. Outdoor restaurants along the Grand Canal are decorated with strings of white lights, hundreds of them. Cold as it is, the dinner crowd is there.

You go to Venice during the winter for Carnevale. The men dress in black capes and tricon hats and white masks that have no expression. He hopes she will be there near the Basilica in Piazza San Marco. He hopes she will be hurt only enough to let him know he was loved.

Ant Life

SHE BATHES TOO much and thinks too much about babies, those perfect hands, those perfect feet. Renee has to fill the tub with steaming water and scrub herself until her skin bleeds. She miscarried the week before last. This happened at the end of her first trimester. Off and on she had prayed for God to take the baby. Now Renee is noticing the neighborhood mothers. They push their baby strollers up and down her street and talk to their babies. Some mothers park their strollers and talk to other mothers and other babies. How lovely, they say. How truly perfect, they say. Renee must lock herself in the bathroom and press her hands over her ears to stop all the talking mothers.

ANTS ARE IN her kitchen sink and not big red ants or big black ants but the tiny black ones that people kill with a fingertip. Renee is leaning her arms on the sink to watch the ants. This evening she fixed her hair in a loose ponytail. Blond strands keep touching her eyelashes. The scabs that once covered her knees and and thin arms and forehead have given her fresh pink skin. Blue veins crisscross her arms and legs. Now the ants are climbing a sugar cube Renee dropped in the sink less than five minutes ago. They are next to the dinner dishes and the glass tumblers and the silverware crusted with food. Florescent lights glare down and the corners of the small kitchen have no shadows. An after dinner smell of roasted chicken is mixed with lavender air freshener. Her husband reaches past her for the faucet. Renee thinks Benjamin will wash the ants into the drain.

She stops him and says, "Are you crazy? How would you like somebody to drown you? Ants are living, breathing creatures," she says. "Doesn't that thought ever occur to you, Benjamin?"

Her jaw clicks when she talks. The jaw was wired shut until last week but it did not set right. Other things are wrong. The bruise on her bottom lip won't disappear. Her forehead and right cheek have scars. Her right arm was fractured at the humerus and the lower part of the radius. The arm healed but the pain refuses to quit and let her sleep.

"They're just ants," Benjamin says. He is tall and mostly angles and bones. His dark hair has started to go thin. Renee can see his bald spot when Benjamin bends over to tie his shoes in the morning. Benjamin is explaining to her how ants breed and can take over a home. He talks for three or four minutes. The lecture has pauses, sighs. Renee thinks he is looking at her like she is from the planet Neptune. Benjamin works as a research biologist for a chemical company in Center City Phil-adelphia and knows what ants do. Renee nudges him away with her hip.

"I'm not stupid," she tells him.

HIS FOOTSTEPS WERE part of the evening traffic. The foot-steps stopped and started to her rhythm. Renee didn't catch on at first. She started listening to his footsteps when the streets became smaller and the hour later and the traffic less. Then Renee turned to see who was there.

"Following me, are you?" Renee said this to him as a joke but a joke that wanted an answer.

Cars passed them, the headlights long and bright. A green and yellow bus waited at the corner next to the white circle of a street light. The air smelled of exhaust fumes from the bus and frying meat from a nearby restaurant.

"We should have another drink," the man said. He laughed and glanced around.

He wouldn't look at her. His hair was brown and clipped neat and parted on the left. He wore cinnamon cologne. Ev-erything about the man was neat, his suit, his starched shirt, his tie centered just so. They had gone to the once a month P.T.A. meeting, that was part of their job. After the meeting Renee and the man decided to have a drink to put away the day.

Renee knows this man very well.

They teach at James Buchanan Elementary on Walnut

Street. They usually drink morning coffee together in the second floor teacher's lounge. Two sugars and no cream for him. They like telling stories about their spouses and their students and what they had watched on TV last night. The man enjoys an intelligent game show. He also has a seven year old named Zachary.

BABIES ON TELEVISION are fat and pink or fat and tan. Television babies play with kittens and puppies and crawl on clean white rugs. They sit in highchairs and open their mouths wide for spoonfuls of puree apricots and peaches. They lay in playpens and discover their toes. They talk in their own language to people and animals that nobody can see. Renee has tried switching television channels, one after another, but the happy babies are everywhere. Television babies come with television mothers. The mothers like to smile unless they are suffering from allergies or migraines or cramps. The babies sit beside their mothers and pat their mother's arms and wait for them to smile again. Now Renee is recording her TV shows so she can fast forwards through the babies.

"THEY'RE ANTS," BENJAMIN says again. He whispers this and touches her back. Renee leans away from him. Benjamin's hand is stranded in space with nothing to do. Things are better, he says. His hand vanishes into the front pocket of his chinos as if her back was an inconsequential detour.

Renee does not want Benjamin embracing her or touching

her. Renee isn't sure what she wants or what she should do about things. It's illogical, she thinks. No, more than that. Illogical is too kind a word, too understated. Who'd wish their unborn baby dead? she thinks. What sort of person has three baths a day? Benjamin should fine a nice sane woman. Renee's doctor has prescribed both an antidepressant and something for her anxiety. One night Benjamin woke her up to hold her and she screamed.

"You were telling jokes at dinner," Benjamin says. "You were doing good, right? Was that my imagination or were you doing good?"

Benjamin is next to Renee who is still looking at the tiny black ants climbing the sugar cube in the kitchen sink. It's amazing to Renee that people squash tiny living things all the time and don't care one way or the other. And God forbid you should confront a person. God forbid you should say, Those ants are living beings. Just because something is small doesn't mean you can stomp it to death.

Benjamin hunches over the counter, his arms on the beige Formica. The florescent lights are too intense for the small kitchen. A window is half open above the sink but the smell of the lavender air freshener and the roasted chickenwon't go away.

Renee knows she hasn't been fair to Benjamin. He wants her to see him as a nonchalant guy who is okay with everything. Benjamin is wearing tan loafers and no socks with his chinos. The sleeves of his blue shirt are rolled to the elbow. Nonchalant. He has the look of a tall, gaunt friar.

"You can talk to me," Benjamin says.

Benjamin and Renee have known each other forever, since their days at Germantown High School. They were married eight years ago last month.

"I know I can talk to you," Renee says. Her voice is small, flimsy.

She keeps staring at the tiny black ants on the sugar cube. Renee and Benjamin cannot have a baby. Benjamin had to go through radiation therapy for testicular cancer. That happened the first year of their marriage. The cancer has remitted but children aren't an option.

"Lots of babies in this world need parents," Renee's mama says.

Her mama has dark brown eyes that can quiet a person's heart with a single look. She tells people to call her Mama Flora. Mama Flora is a small woman with thick legs and big breasts. Renee has her mama's gray-green eyes, her blond hair. Renee and Benjamin love Mama Flora but they have resisted adopting a baby. They don't want any gene pool surprises.

"I wish I smoked," Renee says. "We smoked when we were first married. Remember? I'd go to the little grocery store on the corner and buy us a couple packs of menthols and a chocolate bar with almonds."

Benjamin tries to brush something from Renee's lower back. Rene dodges his hand as if it's electric.

"You know I love you, right?" Benjamin says. His voice is quiet and calm. Then he says, "You know that hasn't changed."

THE GREEN AND yellow bus at the corner was pulling away. Gears shifted and gray smoke and fumes curled into a clear night. The luminous circle from street light drifted across the ads and pictures on the side of the bus. A giant woman with wide blue eyes and thick red lips held an open tube of lipstick next to her face. The bus turned right at the corner and was lost to the dark street, the smoke and the fumes.

"I have a one drink limit," Renee said to the man. She had gone from being amused to not being amused at all. Parts of her were quivering, her shoulders, her thin hands. She squeezed her hands into fists to stop the quivering and stuffed her fists into the pockets of her black satin windbreaker. "I had my one drink," Renee said. She was looking at the street light. "That's my rule," she said.

"You don't break the rules?" the man said. He tried to look at her and smile but he could not look at her for long. His smile was more of a smirk. The man touched the knot of his tie and his starched collar. Isn't that what people do? he said. Don't people break the rules?

"Not tonight," Renee told him and tucked a strand of blond hair behind her ear. She wanted to sound both friendly and firm. She heard the jitter in her voice.

"I think we will," he said. One hand was in his pocket, rattling change.

"Will what?" Renee said and did not know what he meant. The man grabbed her arm with his free hand before she could think.

"You're going to rub your skin away, girl." That's what Mama Flora had said. She was looking over her gold half-shelled glasses at the scrubbed red skin on Renee's arm.

Mama Flora was wearing her blue dress with the big white flowers. Renee and her mama were sitting next to each other on the sectional corduroy sofa in Renee's living room. Renee had recently bought a corduroy recliner to put across from the sectional. Everything about Mama Flora was broad and fleshy. She smelled of sugar cookies. That day Renee told her mama how she had wished her baby dead. Mama Flora looked at Renee and grinned. She had quit cigarettes fifteen years ago but her teeth were yellowed from the smoke and nicotine.

"You can't wish a baby dead, Mama Flora said. "If that were so, hon, you would have been gone at thirteen. If you remember, it was touch and go between us."

"Why can't we have a baby?" Renee says. She knows the answer but wants to hear the question out loud.

The sugar cube is melting in the kitchen sink, a tiny sandy island. The ants are slipping off the wet edge. Renee cannot talk to Benjamin and look at him at the same time. It's like laughing and crying at the same time. It's like rubbing your stomach and patting your head. Some of the black ants float and wiggle in the sugar water. Renee imagines herself small enough to watch the ants drown.

"I want a regular life," Renee says. She knows what she is going to say now before she says it. Renee has said all this before but that does not matter. She hates herself when she says what she is about to say but that doesn't matter, either. "Women actually get pregnant without breaking their bones," Renee says and her shoulders start to shake. "Why do I get the broken bones? What sort of joke is that?"

"You should have married someone else," Benjamin says. He is still standing next to Renee, his back against the beige Formica counter, his pale long arms folded and resting on his chest. The sleeves of his blue cotton shirt are rolled to the elbow. "You should have married a guy whose balls don't glow in the dark," he says.

"That's not what I mean," Renee says. She stiffens her shoulders to stop the quivering but that doesn't help.

"I'm just saying," he says.

The open window does nothing to end the smell of the roasted chicken and the lavender air freshener. Renee's stomach is getting flippy. And that's not the only thing. The fluorescent lights are too intense for the kitchen. She doesn't understand why Benjamin can't buy appropriate kitchen lighting. How difficult is that? she thinks. You go to a hardware store and you tell the salesperson you want lights for a certain sized kitchen. People buy kitchen lighting every day.

RENEE FELT HER arm crack right away. The man had shoved her down and she landed on the wet bricks in the alley. A bare white light bulb hung above each of the two metal doors. One door belonged to the restaurant. Dark green plastic bags were pilled into the trash cans and the rusted dumpster next to the wall. The alley stank of rotting food and frying meat. Kitchen staff had probably hosed off the ground next to the trash cans and the dumpster earlier in the evening. A half moon and the two electric lights reflected on the wet brick and the pools of water. The man with the suit and the starched shirt had grabbed Renee by the hair and hit her forehead against the brick. She saw her blood drift into the water. Bright specks flashed in her eyes. Then nothing. Then time had gone. She didn't know how long she had been unconscious. She smelled his cinnamon cologne and the rotting food and the frying meat. The man was on top of Renee, her jeans and panties to her knees. His talk was breathy, saying how he might beat her again if she told anyone. How he might hurt her bad. How he might do a lot of things, it depended. Was she a good girl? Did she know how to say yes sir and no sir? This was the man Renee had coffee with in the second floor teacher's lounge each morning. Two sugars and no cream. Then he slapped her so hard her jaw snapped. He liked quiz shows and had a seven year old named Zachary. The Man stood and zipped himself and took a black comb from the inside pocket of his suitcoat and raked it through his hair. He removed a white folded handkerchief and rub her from his lips. The man warned her not to follow him or call his home. "I don't need some crazy bitch stalking me," he said.

She had not understood him. The pain was too disruptive. Renee could not open her mouth to ask him what he had meant by not following him or calling his home. She didn't understand the comment about some crazy bitch stalking him. Did the man think she wanted a second date?

HER BATHS ARE always hot. The little mirror above the sink and the black and white bathroom tiles must be damp with steam. Renee washes herself twice a day, occasionally three times a day. She scrubs her breasts and her belly and the sides of her neck. She scrubs between her legs and her inner thighs and between the cheeks of her buttocks. Renee bathes too much and thinks about babies too much. She used to think about becoming a mother and the baby inside of her. Now it's all about other mothers and other babies.

RENEE'S ARMS REST on the rim of the beige kitchen sink. Her shoulders are hunched, her hands locked together by thin fingers.

"I'll take care of the dishes," she says this to Benjamin who is standing beside her. Benjamin is leaning against the Formica counter, arms folded to his chest. The sleeves of his blue cotton shirt are rolled to the elbow. Renee wants him to watch the news in the living room and leave her alone. The sugar cube she had dropped into the sink less than ten minutes ago has melted. The black ants float in a filmy layer of water near the drain. Renee cannot stop the quivering in her shoulders and hands.

"How about I help you with the dishes," Benjamin says.

"That's all right," she says. "I'm good." The fluorescent lights are too intense. She has to squint to see the ants.

"No, seriously," he says.

Benjamin had questioned her at the hospital.

"What does he look like?" Benjamin said. "Is he a stranger or someone you know?"

Renee told him what she had told the police. It was too dark and she was too scared.

"Everything happened really fast," Renee said.

The smell of roasted chicken and lavender air freshener is still strong in the kitchen. Renee's stomach has begun to cramp. Nausea squirms at the back of her throat. Suppose she tells Benjamin the man's name, then what? What would he do? she thinks. He won't buy a gun and shoot him. Benjamin is not a killer. Benjamin won't fight him, either. Renee can't recall her husband ever fighting anyone. And going to the police is a bad idea. She has read what lawyers do to women. Lawyers like to confuse the victim with the perpetrator. How were you dressed? they say. How did you act toward the defendant? they say. Were you provocative? How many men have you had sexual relations with in the past month? The past year? In your life?

Renee can't stop the shaking in her body. Her body has expelled her. It is controlling itself. The eyes become hot and wet and her vision goes haywire. The tiny black ants that float near the drain have blurred. Dinner dishes have blurred, too. The glass tumblers, the silverware crusted with food.

"Oh my Jesus," she says. Her chest swells and flutters. Renee cannot find her breath. She inhales but nothing is there. "Oh my Jesus," she says. Her legs turn fragile then start to fold.

"Easy, easy," Benjamin says.

One arm catches her and circles her shoulders. His free hand reaches for the faucet. Steam and water rush into the sink and begin covering the stacked dinner dishes, the tumblers and silverware. The black ants are motionless and travel on the curl of water into the drain.

Renee's eyes blink open like a doll abruptly righted. She begins striking at him with her fists. He has both arms around her now. Renee is twisting inside his embrace.

"What are you doing?" she says and hears her own panic. She tries to push him from her.

"They're ants," Benjamin says.

"I don't know you," Renee says and pushes at him again. "I thought I did, I thought I knew you. Get away, Benjamin. I mean it."

Benjamin won't let go.

"I am not him," he says. "I'm not that man. His mouth is close to her ear. "Listen to me," he says. "We grew up together. I've loved you since we were kids," he says and his voice is a whisper. He tells her it is time to quit this. "Stop giving your life to him," Benjamin says. "You're giving him more than he took. We are each other's home, you and me. You know that."

She does not want to think about what was taken, what is left. The pain hooks in deep and stay too long, that broken feeling, that shame. Her arms are weighted and fall to her sides. Fists loosen into weary fingers. Benjamin is telling her that maybe he cannot do this and maybe cannot do that but he can hold her. "I'm good for a few things," he says and pats her back with the flat of his hand.

Renee's forehead presses to his chest, his soft blue cotton shirt. She is tired and her once fractured arm has started to burn. Every part of her aches in the evening. The body won't forget. That's what the doctor told her. Renee feels Benjamin's hand rubbing her back.

"Shh, shh," he says.

The florescent glare is too bright for their small kitchen. She cannot find comfort under this light. There are never enough shadows.

The Last Time I Came Home To You

He was drinking his second glass of Pinot and listening as two Frenchmen talked about robbing an old woman. This evening had a chill and carried the smell of onion and frying beef from the restaurant next door. The two men were sitting behind Preston Ellis outside the Café Fleur Bleu on the Place St.-Michel. One of the men said the old woman owned the Tunisian pastry shop across the street near the Metro. Both Frenchmen were quiet but not quiet enough. Preston Ellis had passed the two men on the way to his table. The small round tables had blue roses painted on white Formica tops and the chairs were white wicker with blue trim. Preston Ellis knew the one with the mustache and the bad skin had the thick smoker's voice. That voice was speaking now. The other Frenchman wore his dark hair short with sideburns and had not talked at all. When Preston Ellis passed the two men the one with the sideburns was nodding to the other one and pressing his big knuckles into his palm. The old woman who owned the Tunisian pastry shop was also a money lender. That was what the man with the smoker's voice said. The old woman kept close to thirty thousand euros in a strong box at the back of the store behind a gray curtain that hid a bed and a kitchenette.

"Are you truly sure, Robert?" the man with the sideburns said. "I don't need problems."

Robert said he was very truly sure. He knew people who knew people. Reliable people.

A THUNDER STORM came to the desert early that first morning. After the storm the clouds turned thready and white and the sun burned away the rain. Preston Ellis had been thinking about his trip to the desert before the two Frenchmen at the table behind him began discussing how they would rob the old woman. He was thinking, *I did not see the city until after I felt the heat and smelled the sulphur coming off the Tigris and the Euphrates.* The desert had tanned him, his long skinny legs, his arms like brown vines. Even the wind was hot. Wind rolled the sand over the gray tar streets. He thought, *My wife said I was crazy. How can you film a war that isn't there?* she wanted to know. What war? she said. What war are you filming? My wife was angry that I bought a six thousand dollar camera. She was angry that I taped ten thousand dollars to my leg. Last year Preston Ellis and his wife had traveled from Richmond, Virginia to Paris. His wife was a painter. She had accepted an adjunct position at the Sorbonne which left her time to paint. They had not been out of school for very long. The expensive camera and the ten thousand was added to their loan. Preston Ellis understood her anger

but needed the camera to do his work and the money to bribe his way into a war that would start soon. Seven months into his documentary his wife's unpaid bills appeared, rent, utilities, credit cards. He could not reach his wife by phone and she would not answer his email. That was when he had to stop his work in the desert and come back to Paris.

ACROSS THE STREET from the Café Fleur Bleu, people were coming out of the Metro onto the Place St.-Michel. The sky had gone dark except for a pink scar where the sun had left the evening. Tall Birch trees crossed the moon and brought shadows to the street. A white dog sat near the entrance way to the Metro with its back straight and its front paws together as if it were a very proper dog. Preston Ellis and the white dog watched each other. There had been a dog in the desert like the one by the Metro but the one in the desert had pronounced ribs and dirty white fur. Headlights from cars and buses showed the people in silhouette. Paris traffic did not have an odor. Preston Ellis had noticed this from day one. You could smell the food and the perfume but you could not smell the traffic.

"We should do this tonight," the man with the tobacco voice was saying in French. He said, "Friday is the best time."

Preston Ellis thought the two men at the table behind

him were actors rehearsing something. He did not know any actors personally. What he knew were movies where actors rehearsed their parts while drinking wine or coffee at a café. Now the one named Robert with the bad skin and the smoker's voice was saying, People go in and out of the old woman's shop all day Friday to give her loan payments. You would not know the woman has money. To look at her I mean. She hides her success. Nobody would know, an old woman like that.

Preston Ellis sipped his glass of Pinot and listened to the two men. He imagined robbing the old woman. The thirty thousand euros could pay our debits and give us extra, he thought. Maybe his wife would not be so depressed. Preston Ellis believed his wife was having an affair with one of her students. David. Fondly, David. That was how the student had signed his note. Fondly, David. Possibly she did not love him and nothing was going on. Or maybe next week the student would write a note to a different woman.

Who can know another person's heart?

His wife's name was Maureen but he called her Moe. She was short with narrow hips and a tiny waist and cropped black hair. Moe had large green eyes and watched everything he did. *It's the money*, Preston Ellis thought. It's being alone and it's the money. She is an artist, an emotional person. She isn't good at paying bills or caring for herself. Moe had miscarried when they were juniors at Virginia Commonwealth and tried to kill herself. Preston Ellis wanted to do what was right.

"Let me take care of you," he had told her. "We get along, don't we?"

The way he loved the desert and the war had surprised him. He did not want to leave his work. Preston Ellis once told his wife that his work was no different than her work. Moe looked at him with those large green eyes like he was crazy. If I can get the money she will be all right, this was what Preston Ellis believed. He wondered if the two Frenchmen sitting at the table behind him were actors or robbers.

THE BULLET HOLES were small dark circles in a white wall. Sockets without the eyes, he thought. No one could forget the desert, no one who worked or fought there. The bullets had entered at angles and blew out the plaster. Wedges. Shards. Bullets had cut into the pink and green floral curtains that covered the glass doors leading to the balcony. The glass shattered but would not collapse. There were holes in the glass and there were concaved cobwebs that glitter like a coin tossed under a desert sun. His apartment smelled of Scotch and gun powder and the clothes he never washed. I did not have a minute to hang my jacket in the closet, Preston Ellis thought. Clothes laid on the concrete floor beside an open brown and green suitcase next to the mattress. Soldiers told him to sleep low to the floor.

"Use just the mattress," the soldiers had said.

"I cannot remember a time when I did not want to do what I am doing now in the desert. I am my best when I am doing my work." Preston Ellis had emailed this to his wife at the end of his first month. He had written, "I am filming my documentary between freelancing for three US cable networks and an Italian network. My French is a lot better than my Italian but no one has complained. One day I am in Umm Qasr and the next day I am in Al Kut outside of Baghdad. I hope you are getting the money. There is enough to pay the rent and the other bills and whatever you might need. This is no easy dollar. People say you become shorter on luck the longer you are here."

COILED HEATERS WERE beneath the awnings at the Café Fleur Bleu. Preston Ellis felt both the warmth of the heaters and the chilled Paris night. On the boulevard and to the left was the fountain where Saint Michel stood with his sword raised above the dragon. Water from the fountain tumbled and showed the moonlight and the shadows of the Birch trees. Preston Ellis looked across the street for the white dog by the Metro but the dog had left without a good-bye. The two men behind Preston Ellis were smoking cigarettes. A breeze rushed the cigarette smoke around him. He brushed the smoke away with the back of his hand then took a sip of the Pinot.

"We can use the window next to the rear door," the smoker's voice said.

He was still talking about stealing the thirty thousand euros from the woman who owned the Tunisian pastry shop, the money lender.

The other man with the dark short hair and the sideburns smoked and kept quiet. Preston Ellis heard them exhaling their cigarettes.

"It's a small window but big enough for me," the man with the smoker's voice said. "I'll crawl in and open the door."

He was whispering and certain words like 'stealing' and 'thirty thousand' were said softly and in English. Preston Ellis was taller than the man who was speaking but thin enough for the window. *Hips, chest, shoulders, we're the same*, he thought.

Now the man with the dark short hair and the sideburns was talking.

"Early in the morning," he was saying. "Maybe one or two. What do you think, Robert?"

The man who had the smoker's voice laughed at this. The laugh was throaty and became a cough.

"That should be fine," he said in French. "I can feel the money in my pocket. That is always my good luck sign."

THREE DAYS AGO Preston Ellis had searched his wife's closet and bureau. Peach colored drapes billowed about the open bedroom window. Moe had bought the drapes at a shop off the Rue des Grands Degres in the Latin Quarter where they lived. The air from the window was cool and the fragrance of new bread from the downstairs bakery came into the room on a breeze. He had thought, Show me something. Everyone leaves clues, the bill from a cell phone, a credit card receipt, a matchbook with the name of a restaurant I don't know.

Clues were inevitable. His wife had changed in ways Preston Ellis could not explain right away. He saw the change on his first day home. She had allowed him to hold her but she was more the good child tolerating his touch than the wife who had waited for that touch. Her large green eyes watched everything except him.

And when wives change what do husbands do?

His fingers probed the wool sweaters in her bureau, the cotton sweaters, her folded slips and bras and panties. The panties were silk with neon colors and laid beside each other like melting sherbets. Preston Ellis had searched places he should have left alone and he thought of conversations he did not need to recall.

"Your body is put together in an odd way," Moe used to tell him that. They had been together for four years, married for two. "Your head is too small for your torso," she'd tell him. He had disproportionate arms and very pronounced white knees. His face was narrow and his cheekbones were high and well cut but his eyes were weasel eyes. Moe evaluated him without mercy. "God built you from leftover parts," Moe would say.

The day before he had searched her closet and the cherry wood bureau he had found a Thank You card folded and tossed into the plastic trash can beside the kitchen table. This was the sort of plain white card someone might attach to flowers or chocolates.

The card read, "To my favorite American instructor, thank you for all your help. I never thought I could love my language with a Virginia accent. Fondly, David." The ink was black and the handwriting had a confident stroke. Fondly, David.

Preston Ellis read the Thank You card many times.

The two Frenchmen had paid their bill and walked past Preston Ellis toward the bridge where the Boulevard St.-Michel became the Boulevard du Palais. The Seine was black and smooth and the lights from the buildings and a half moon were gold on the river. Preston Ellis poured the last of the Pinot from the carafe into his glass. Many people were out now. The French ate dinner late, 9:30, 10:00. The smell of meat and fish and onion was tacked to a breeze and the chilled night air. He swallowed the Pinot and looked at his watch. 10:36. The two men would be back in three or four hours to rob the money lender. Preston Ellis imagined them crossing the boulevard near the fountain on Place St.-Michel and going into the alley next to the Tunisian pastry shop. The one with the mustache and bad skin would crawl through the small window and unlock the door for the other one.

I could be there and gone, Preston Ellis thought. *And why not? I could have the thirty thousand euro in my pocket before midnight.* He saw himself arranging the euros in neat stacks on the white kitchen table. *I will have flowers on the table, too, certainly flowers, he thought, roses or maybe lilies. I will have a note on a white card that ends with, All my love, Preston. We can make this a celebration. You must close your eyes*, Preston Ellis imagined telling his wife. *Hold my hand and close your eyes.*

A DOG PATTED along the empty gray tar street next to the desert. Hot wind blew sand about the dog and over the street. The dog blinked and shook itself. Ribs showed beneath dirty white fur. Rusted cars had been abandoned here and there. Several cars were no more than charred frames and tires that had melted. There was the stench of burnt rubber. The dog held a hand in its mouth. Its teeth gripped the bruised wrist. The hand was swollen and black and the hard skin had cracked along the side of the palm. Preston Ellis wanted to start his documentary with the dog carrying the hand. He had watched the film clip over and over on the monitor of his camera, that bony dog with the hand in its mouth. Each time he watched the clip his thought was the same. *Whose hand were you?* he would say to himself. The wind was very strong and the sand was thrashing the dog. More than once the dog had to stop and lower its head to the sand and the wind. But the dog did not let go of the hand.

"Whose hand were you?" Preston Ellis had said out loud.

The dog looked weak and its legs were thin and shaky. Its ribs pressed tight against dirty white fur. A constant wind and the blowing sand had caused the dog to stumble. The dog had stumbled many times. But the dog did not let go of the hand.

"Whose hand were you?" Preston Ellis had whispered again.

He would start his documentary with the wind blowing sand over the empty street and the bony dog carrying the hand.

"There are discoveries here." Preston Ellis wrote this in his last email to his wife. "Have you ever said to yourself, 'This is the only thing I can do? This is the only place I can be?' There are secrets on the side of the road. And what is more important than that?" he wrote her. "You tell me, Moe. I will listen to you. I am all ears, tell me."

THE BREEZE WAS cold now and flapped the white and pale blue awning of the café. Small coiled heaters under the awning gave warmth but could not stop the cold. Preston Ellis propped the empty carafe on the bill for the Pinot and his twenty Euros to keep all of it from flying off into the night. An older woman passed him on the way to a table. She had an angular delicate face with swept back gray-brown hair and gold earrings. Cinnamon and orange perfume trailed her. Preston Ellis nodded to the woman and started walking toward a traffic light at the Place St.-Michel. He was thinking about Fondly Dave and the folded note written in black ink and a confident stroke. Earlier in the day Preston Ellis had stood across the street from the university on the Rue des Ecoles to wait for his wife. *To spy on her*, he thought. Call it what it was. To spy on her. Gray clouds had marked the sky after a quick afternoon rain. He was pretending to look for a scarf at a souvenir shop when he saw his wife and a young man he did not know on the front steps of the university. The young man had on a waist-length black leather jacket and his hair was long and fixed in a ponytail. Preston Ellis's wife was looking up at him and smiling. Her large green eyes watched his face. The young man had leaned down and kissed Preston Ellis's wife on the lips. His kiss seemed more obligation than passion. The young man smiled back at her and started to go but she was still holding his arm.

THE PARIS NIGHT was cold now and the breeze moved the branches and the leaves of the Birch trees along the boulevard St.-Michel. Preston Ellis had crossed the street to have a closer look at the Tunisian pastry shop. Perhaps he would go down the alley to see the small window beside the back door. He tried to picture himself arranging the old woman's euros in neat stacks on his kitchen table but the images would not stay in his mind. Moonlight went between the leaves of the trees and was bright over the pavement. Pastries filled the glass front of the old woman's shop. There were glazed fruit tarts, dates stuffed with chocolate and almond paste, round and square donuts with cream centers, pine nut and pistachio Halkooms, teakwood trays of uncut fudge. Preston Ellis put his hand to the glass. The display lights were hot on his palm. His eyes started to burn and tear and his chest opened to an empty feeling that snatched his breath. Then the traffic became too noisy. Horns were loud and too long. People had started shouting things. Preston Ellis turned toward the street when he noticed a reflection of the white dog he had seen earlier near the Metro. It was trotting down the center of the Boulevard St.-Michel, oblivious to all the horns and shouting. The animal moved like it knew where it was going and what it was going to do when it got there. The white dog was heading for the bridge to the Ile de la Cite, where the Boulevard St.-Michel became the Boulevard du Palais. Preston Ellis raised his hand and waved, tentatively, slowly, as if to signal an old friend in a different wilderness.

Their Days Before Maine

THERE WERE UNDER the breath remarks about Jorgie's clothes and his haircut and the secrets his face gave away. He was sitting where the new sixth grade boys sat when they didn't need grief and couldn't get invisible. Mrs. Dover called his name. She had gray ear-length hair and a small dark red mouth and bony fingers with clear nail polish. She glanced up from the class roster to look for a raised hand. Mrs. Dover called for him again. She said his name like a question she could take or leave.

"Jorgie-Porgie," a boy said.

Then another kid giggled. Jorgie hunched down in the new boy's chair. The chair was near the window, near the girl with the green eyes and the skinny legs.

"My name is Evelyn," she whispered and showed Jorgie a smile.

HIS MOTHER PROTECTED him by unplugging the television

and hiding the radio and not letting him read magazines and newspapers.

"I don't want you too stimulated," his mother told him. "You're a brooder like me," she said. "We're cursed that way. Believe me, all this brooding isn't healthy, not for a young boy and not for a mama."

Last week they moved from their Philadelphia townhouse on Rittenhouse Square to Norfolk, Virginia. His mother had picked Norfolk by shutting her eyes and tapping her finger on a map.

"We're starting over," that's what she kept saying. "You and me, Jorgie, we're starting a new life and finding new friends."

Bruna Mendoza was shorter than her son and thicker about the waist. Both Bruna and Jorgie had black hair and brown lazy eyes. They were pretty people. Jorgie was slim and tall and his mom was beefy but with a good shape. They also had pretty white teeth thanks to Jorgie's father. A month ago Dr. Mendoza left his family for a dental hygienist.

The two of them ran off and bought a farm in Maine.

Jorgie didn't want to start over and he didn't want new friends. He stayed in his bedroom and read. Yesterday he had read an article about spontaneous combustion. The article said there were people who walked down the street and exploded. No warning, no headache or sick feeling came with it, no nothing, just boom. You were alive then you were embers and ash. Who wanted to start over if people exploded and fathers ran off to Maine with strangers?

Jorgie's bedroom had one grimy white wall covered in blue and orange crayon smiley faces and houses with thin curls of smoke and animals that had circles for bodies and stick legs and big teeth. The other three walls were water stained near the ceiling. The brown carpet was spotty and smelled of cigarettes and pee.

"Don't you worry," Mrs. Mendoza said. "A little paint, some carpet, we'll fix it up. It'll be fun, Jorgie, hon. No sense wasting what money we have on a fancy place." This afternoon his mother had on her silver silk kimono and was sitting in Jorgie's mahogany desk chair with one plump leg tucked under her and the other leg stretched out. She liked her stockings rolled below the knee and shoes that slipped on and had a low square heel. "You'll see," Mrs. Mendoza said. "You can pick your own color for the walls and pick the carpet, too. Just wait, Jorgie. You're going to have some showcase." His mother was smoking a Parliament and holding a small blue metal ashtray.

Jorgie's furniture didn't belong in this room. The mahogany bureau and desk set, the sleigh bed and the nightstand, these pieces were built by his father and seemed out of place here. The room and his furniture were strangers to one another. They were together by circumstance instead of choice. The room reminded him of the dirty homeless men he used to see begging for quarters outside the train station in downtown Philly.

His mother was talking to him about their new next door neighbors. Pastor Bob or Bill and his daughter.

"A fascinating, delightful girl, Jorgie" His mother's poked the air twice with the two fingers holding her cigarette. "And very attractive. Your age and a real charmer. Evelyn, maybe, or Eve. No, Evelyn. Mrs. Mendoza nodded at her last choice and took a drag on her cigarette and patted the ash into the blue metal ashtray. His mother said, "You're one lucky kid."

JORGIE DIDN'T TELL his mother that the new girl had walked home with him from Granby Elementary. Evelyn was slim and an inch taller than Jorgie and wore a jeans skirt and sneakers without socks. She had brown and blond hair fixed in a braid that ended at the small of her back. Silver rings covered her thumbs and fingers and silver bracelets covered her thin wrists. When Evelyn walked she made a sound like coins in a pocket. Jorgie thought she smelled good, too. Talcum powder and watermelon. But the best part about Evelyn was her smile and those even white teeth. His father would have loved her teeth.

Jorgie imagined his father saying, "Good work, Jorgie, a girl with teeth like that can do no wrong."

"I live with daddy and his brother," Evelyn had said.

Her mom died two years ago. Pneumonia or TB or a mixture of both, Evelyn was not sure. Her dad was Pastor Bob and her dad's brother was an A-hole named Delbert James who drank too much and had shot her dog. The dog was a black and white border collie called Gypsy. Delbert shot the dog in the right front leg and now Gypsy walked with a limp.

"Delbert's very nervous," Evelyn said. "Every time he gets angry his eyes shake like they're cold."

Jorgie knew why he hadn't told his mother about Evelyn. He didn't want to talk about Delbert James shooting the dog.

A PHOTOGRAPH OF Belinda the dental hygienist was in a cardboard box labeled His Stuff in red letters. Jorgie had found the photograph while sneaking a look at his father's things. There were old brown pipes with black bowls and a leather carry pouch with two cigars in clear plastic tubes. There were six detective paperbacks and a novel by Gabriel Garcia Marquez. There was a pair of worn brown leather slippers and a chunky Swiss Army penknife and the blue and cream colored mask of a woman that Dr. Mendoza had bought in Venice. Belinda's photograph was under the papier-mâché mask. She sat on a dark green wingback chair with her hands folded in her lap and her feet together, a prissy, stiff pose. Jorgie thought she was old but not as old as his mother and no way near as old as his father. She seemed old enough, though, twenty-five, maybe twenty-eight. Belinda looked the opposite of his mother. She was tall and delicate and had wide open eyes and straight blond hair past her shoulders.

"This isn't your business," his father said. He laid on the mahogany sleigh bed with his short legs crossed at the ankles.

Or Jorgie imagined it.

Mrs. Mendoza didn't need to unplug the television and hide the radio. Right now Jorgie was imagining his father in a green velour sweatsuit and wearing white jogging shoes. Dr. Mendoza's thinning black hair was dyed to hide the gray and slicked back. He held an unlighted cigar between the thumb and forefinger of his right hand. A diamond ring with a gold band was on his little finger.

"Sometimes we choose good and bad at the same time," his father said. "I miss you and love you, Jorgie, but I love Belinda. What am I supposed to do? You'll understand when you fall in love."

"You're a father," Jorgie said. "You're not supposed to go to Maine."

"Belinda's parents live in Maine," his father said and rolled the thick unlighted cigar between his thumb and forefinger. Then he said, "Doesn't your mother always say how people have to compromise in a relationship?"

"This isn't what normal parents do," Jorgie said. "You can't stop being somebody's father. It's not like a hobby. It's not like you're giving up golf for tennis. Don't you know anything?"

"Maybe I love Belinda more than you," his father said. "Haven't you ever thought, 'My dad loves her more than me?' Doesn't your mother say that to you, Jorgie? Doesn't she say, 'Oh, daddy just loves that Belinda more than us. We're just yesterday's news to your daddy. You and I need to forget all about him, Jorgie.' Doesn't you mother say things like that? Isn't she always telling you how men my age run after younger women like they were lifeboats on the Titanic?"

"It's true, Jorgie," a female voice said. "Your father just loves me more than you, that's all." Belinda the dental hygienist had joined them. She sat on the mahogany desk chair at the opposite end of the bedroom. Belinda said, "Look at this body, Jorgie. Look at these legs. Wouldn't you love me more than you? Wouldn't you love me more than your mother? Your mother is short and fat and wears those dumb kimonos and those dumb shoes with the square heels and smokes cigarettes. God, who wouldn't love me more? I'm young and beautiful and my breath is always fresh. I have chewing gum breath every minute of the day." Belinda was dressed in the clothes she had worn for the photograph. She had on a pleated red and white plaid skirt and a white t-shirt and shiny black high heels with frilly pink and white socks. She said, "Do you want to smell my breath, Jorgie? Come on, Jorgie, smell my wonderful fresh breath."

Belinda the dental hygienist opened her cherry red lips and made a huuh noise and Jorgie could smell her Dentine from across the room.

That was it, that was enough. Jorgie tore away a corner of the photograph, the shiny left high heel and a frilly pink and white sock, the slim right ankle and her lower calf. Both his father and Belinda screamed. Jorgie looked up from the torn photograph. Belinda still had her hands folded in her lap like her picture but now she was staring at her legs. Her shiny left high heel and frilly pink and white sock had disappeared, along with her ankle and her lower calf.

"DELBERT TRIED TO shoot my dog again," Evelyn said. I think he was drunk. I could smell the whiskey. He usually tries to touch me when he's been drinking. He starts feeling brave and all." Evelyn and Jorgie were on their way to school. She said, "You want to carry my books? A boy usually carries his girlfriend's books." Jorgie told her that he liked her but he did not want a girlfriend. She said uh-huh and okay and then she said, "Daddy thinks I ought to have more patience with Delbert. Daddy says Delbert's been in the war and isn't right."

"You mean crazy?" Jorgie said.

"Daddy calls it nervous from the service," Evelyn said.

Clouds had turned the sky a pale charcoal color. A breeze stirred the warm air and the morning smelled of rain that hadn't shown itself.

"What do you mean he touches you?" Jorgie said.

"He touches me," Evelyn said. "Here and here." Her left hand tapped her chest and the crotch of her jeans. Her fingernails were rough and chewed and the red nail polish was chipped. Silver bracelets jingled to the motion of her thin bare arms. Evelyn said, "He can't help himself. That's what he says. He says I'm so pretty he loses control. Do you think I'm pretty, Jorgie?"

"You have beautiful teeth," Jorgie said. "My dad always tells mom and me how he loves beautiful teeth and a beautiful smile. He's an orthodontist and he goes all over the world fixing people's smiles. He once went to England and fixed the queen's smile. Did you ever see the queen smile?"

"Sometimes on TV," Evelyn said.

"My dad did that," Jorgie said.

Mrs. Mendoza opened the bedroom window an inch or two to let in the summer evening and the sound of the crickets. She brushed a strand of black hair away from Jorgie's forehead and kissed him goodnight and told him he was a wonderful boy and that she loved him much more than a person could ever say.

When his mother closed the door, Jorgie sat up in his bed and looked out the window. The night was clear and warm and smelled of boxwood and pine. He could see Evelyn's bedroom but not Evelyn. A rosy yellow light filled her window and colored the white laced curtain. Music came from her room. The music was old fashioned and slow, what his mother called the big bands.

"My mama and dad used to dance to that music," his mother would say. "It's the sweetest. Isn't it the sweetest, Jorgie? Dancing to the big bands is like dancing on air," she liked to say.

Then his mother would dip and glide about the living room in her silk kimono and hum to herself and lift her plump arms like she was dancing with a partner only she could see.

Jorgie wondered if Evelyn had fallen asleep with the light on or if she was reading or maybe talking on the phone. What do you care? he thought. Who cares what some girl is doing, anyway? He imagined crazy Delbert drinking his whiskey and finishing off Evelyn's stupid dog and going after Evelyn. Jorgie told himself to quit thinking. Jorgie told himself that he had his own problems and that he didn't need any new problems and whether or not Delbert was nervous from the service was not a problem he was adding to his list.

Jorgie reached his hand under his pillow and retrieved the eight by ten of Belinda the dental hygienist. The corner piece he had torn from the photograph had been taped back but it was off center.

"Your mother is a wonderful woman," Dr. Mendoza said.

"That makes no sense," Jorgie said. "Why would you leave somebody you thought was wonderful?"

"Our hearts defy logic," his father said.

Jorgie was imagining him in the same green velour sweatsuit and his white jogging shoes. His father stood by the open window. Moonlight pierced the velour and the pores of his face and his hands. Jorgie's bedroom was filled with luminous silver and pools of shadows.

"Your mother is an absolutely wonderful woman," his father said again. "Do you remember me telling you that, Jorgie? I'd say, "now there's a wonderful woman. Loyal, generous. A woman who'd do anything for a person.' And a lovely smile. Doesn't your mother have the loveliest smile? One of my better jobs, you know."

"I thought I was one of your better jobs?" the woman said.

"Exactly how many better jobs did you do?"

"You are my best job," his father said. "You're my masterpiece."

Belinda was across the bedroom, sitting on the mahogany desk chair and giving Dr. Mendoza the evil eye. Shadows camouflaged some of the details but her clothes and how she sat in the chair hadn't changed. She still had the same pose, her hands folded on her lap and her feet together. She still wore the pleated red and white plaid skirt and the white t-shirt and the black high heels with frilly pink and white socks. The only change was the one that matched the torn and repaired photograph. Her lower left calf was off center from her left leg.

"You know what mama says?" Jorgie said to his father.

"I can only imagine," his father said.

"Mama says, 'He gives people beautiful teeth but nothing to make them smile. Nobody wants to smile around him,' that's what mama says. She says, 'You get them all dressed up but they've got nowhere to go.'"

"I have a new life now, Jorgie," his father said. "You should get a new life, too. You stay in this depressing, smelly room. You read your books and hide. Or complain about me. You don't want a girlfriend. You don't want anybody. That's not a life. I don't know what it is but it's not a life. " Moonlight was seeping through Dr. Mendoza's green sweatsuit and the pores of his hands and his face and the pupils of his eyes. "People go away all the time," his father said. "So what. They divorce. They get crazy or sick or crippled. They die. They leave you in a hundred ways. But so what. So what."

Jorgie was watching Belinda in the shadows and the silver light. He tore away a piece of the photograph and saw her left shoulder and part of her red and white plaid skirt disappear. Belinda screamed but her hands stayed folded in her lap and her back was straight. She opened her mouth to scream again and the scream came out a second or two later. Belinda reminded Jorgie of an angry frightened bird.

"Stop this now," his father said to Jorgie and shook a finger at him.

Dr. Mendoza walked over to Belinda and rubbed her back and said, "Shhh, shhh, everything's all right. Everything's fine." Moonlight drained the color from the two of them and left only gray.

Then his father took a new cigar from the pocket of his velour jacket and turned to Jorgie and said, "You know I've been a good father. You know that, Jorgie. What've I always told you? 'Give a man good teeth and a good smile and the world is his oyster,' that's what I've always said. "The Queen of England thanked me for her smile, Jorgie. Can you imagine that? Alejandro Juan Abdo Mendoza was thanked by the Queen of England herself."

"That's something I made up," Jorgie said. "I made it up because you were never home." Both his hands gripped Belinda's photograph like a boy with his finger on the trigger. "You don't know anything," Jorgie said. His chest felt hot and swollen. Jorgie heard his own angry voice. He said,

"You don't see the queen's husband running off to Maine."

"I've given you the two things a man needs to survive in this world," Dr. Mendoza said. He took the thick dark cigar from its plastic tube and sniffed its length and rolled it between his thumb and forefinger. "I've given you good teeth and a good smile," he said. "That's my gift, free of charge. Free to my son."

Jorgie heard his name now.

Evelyn was calling to him in a forceful whisper from her bedroom window.

She called him over the trumpets and drums of the big bands, the pianos and the violins. She called him through the thick air of a summer night.

"Jorgie," she was saying. "Jorgie, can you come to the window? Are you there?"

If his father had said anything else, Jorgie didn't remember. This was the sum of it, all their talks, all their times together, all the days before Maine. Nothing else came to mind. Everything stopped there. Jorgie had just rearranged what he had heard and felt before Belinda and Maine had taken his father.

"But so what," Dr. Mendoza would say.

So what, Jorgie thought.

He had his mother with her silver kimono and her Parliaments and they got along the way they had always gotten along. Jorgie and his mother liked to go see the Phillies in the summer. They had picnics during the spring and the art museum and the zoo during the autumn. There were movies in the winter. Don't forget the movies, lots of movies in the winter, the long, long winter.

What We Do For Love

He had not seen the German photographer in two years but he recognized him right away. The German did not see Walter Rayno at all and would not have known him if he had seen him. The only other time the German had missed seeing Walter Rayno was on the second floor of the Musee d'Orsay when the photographer was taking flash pictures of the Van Goghs.

The German is naked now and duct taped to a Louis XIV chair upholstered in dark blue with gilt Beechwood trim. Afternoon sunlight goes long through the four living room windows of Walter Rayno's apartment on the Rue de Verneuil. The German's legs are thick and freckled and have no hair. Drooping flesh hide his ribs. A rum spice cologne mixes with the stench of bowel and sodium hypochlorite.

Walter Rayno has been filming himself torturing this man. He is younger than the German by thirty years. Walter Rayno likes to wear his gray gabardine and a matching silk tie when he does his work. He has duct taped the German's mouth and taped the eyelids open to let a halogen lamp burn into the pupils. He has shaved the photographer's chest, legs and fleshy arms and rubbed him with the sodium hypochlorite. Color is being bleached from the older man's body.

The German appeared in the background of a two year old photograph Walter Rayno had taken of the then new Mrs. Rayno. The marriage had lasted just under a year and the photograph was rediscovered on a memory card in an old digital camera. She was posed on the steps outside the Musee d'Orsay. Walter Rayno had e-mailed the photo of his ex-wife to a detective service in Paris. Finding the German and renting the apartment had used up most of an already modest trust fund. But worth it at twice the price, that's what Walter Rayno thinks.

THE MUSEE D'ORSAY is on Bellechasse. It's two or three blocks from the apartment Walter Rayno rented last month on the Rue de Verneuil. Before the Musee d'Orsay became a museum it was the Paris terminus for the Orleans railroad company. The ceiling is high and curved and has many tiny rectangular glass panels that let in a steady and even light.

"I think the man should be thrown into a prison." Walter Rayno's new bride had said that about the German photographer.

This was two years ago and the Raynos were in Paris on their honeymoon. They were touring the impressionist collection at the museum. Where the guards were nobody knew. A short man with gray-black hair and a red puffy face was using a flash camera ten or so inches from Van Gogh's *Starry Night*. The man was big about the waist and wore chinos and a pink sweate.

"He should be flogged," she had said. Walter's wife is named Antonette but her parents and her sister call her Tee.

"Nobody's going to flog anybody," Walter Rayno said and patted her shoulder with the flat of his hand and told her to lower her voice.

Tee was finishing a master's in art history at Virginia Commonwealth University in Richmond. Walter was in the M.B.A. program.

"I can't believe the asshole is flashing a Van Gogh," Tee said. "Can you believe that shit? Are the guards on a break? Where are the damn guards when you need them?" Tee had pale bony knees, curled hair the color of teak wood and lips that stayed chapped. Her tortoise shell glasses and thick lenses cover her face like a mask. "That's the *Starry Night*, for Christ-sake," Tee said. Her forefinger finger pushed her glasses to the bridge of her nose. "Go talk to him," she had said to Walter. "Tell him he might as well leave the goddamn picture in Sahara desert and let the sun fry it. Okay? Tell him that."

Impressionists were on the second floor. The Van Gogh room was large and had white walls and track lighting. People sat on glossy wood benches or wandered from picture to picture in a stop and start line. Their perfume and aftershave left the air much too dense and sweet. No velvet ropes marked the distance between the viewers and the paintings and the paintings had no glass cover.

"The French already hate us," Walter Rayno said. He was tall and slim like his new bride but more formally dressed, a dark suit and red striped tie. Tee had on sandals, her ivory blouse and a short pleated skirt. "We are not going to make a scene," he said to her in a whisper. "Let's not be the crass Americans. The French think we're nothing but hillbillies and cowboys."

This was when Tee called her new husband a wimp and walked off to see the Monets.

THE VIDEO CAMERA is attached to a black metal tripod six to seven feet from the German photographer. Duct tape still binds his hands and legs to the Louis XIV chair in the living room of Walter Rayno's apartment on the Rue de Verneuil. The German is still gagged and his eyelids are taped open. Walter Rayno has just shut off the halogen lamp he uses to force heat and brightness into the photographer's eyes. A late afternoon sun stretches light through the four ceiling to floor windows behind the camera. The smell of meat and fish from nearby restaurants drift into the apartment with the sunlight. Traffic sounds have become more urgent. People are beginning to leave their work for the drive home. Walter Rayno is brushing the sleeve of his gray gabardine suit coat and smiling at the camera. He points to the naked German's shoulders, the chest and inner thighs.

These are the areas where the sodium hypochlorite has bleached the skin.

"Right here and here," the young man says to the camera. "This is more than another fair skinned person," he says. What we have is a vanilla ice cream color or the color of mountain snow. In two days the sodium hypochlorite has left his skin totally white," Walter Rayno says and pats the German's arm to compliment him on the good job done so far.

A clear plastic sheet is beneath the Louis XIV chair. Urine and excrement are pooled about the chair's gilt Beechwood legs and the pale bare feet of the German photographer. Walter Rayno begins adhering fresh tape to the German's mouth.

"*Ich bin besorgt. Meine Katzen haben keine Nahrung,*" the German manages to say. His voice is frail and becomes inaudible before he finishes his sentence.

Walter Rayno can speak some French and Italian but does not understand German and wants to know if the older man can speak English. The English is broken and accented.

"I am anxious," the German says. He says, "My cats have no food."

AFTER THEIR TOUR of the Musee d'Orsay Walter Rayno took his new bride for a honeymoon dinner at a neighborhood bistro, *Vins et Terroirs,* on Rue Saint

Andre des Arts close to the Latin Quarter. Small tables were pressed together in a small dark room. Walter ordered a chardonnay and the salmon salad. Tee had a pinot noir and the steamy beef stew with sliced carrots, onions, and russet potatoes. The bistro smelled of beef and fish and warm bread. Couples sat close to Walter Rayno and his new bride but the couples kept to themselves.

"You should have stood up to that photographer," Tee told him and took a sip of the pinot noir. She had ordered a carafe and much of the wine was gone now. A young Englishman in a skinny black wool suit had chased the photographer from the Van Goghs. This annoyed Walter Rayno more than the man with the flash camera. Tee was looking at the white table cloth while she drank the pinot noir and talked. Her narrow face and large tortoise shell glasses were in the shadows. "I'm glad a lady can count on someone," she said.

Walter Rayno believed Tee expected men to take care of her and protect her and do the jobs she wanted to do but found too uncomfortable. She was like a social mutant from the fifties. Most women Tee's age would have walked up to the photographer in the pink sweater and told him to stop using his flash. They might have smashed the camera or slapped the photographer's puffy red face. They would have lectured him about irreplaceable art the way Tee's annoying young Englishman had done. The photographer had gripped his flash camera to his chest, said something nervous in German and escaped the gallery. Walter Rayno was learning that a man could not truly know a woman until he married her.

"There is nothing wrong with a gentleman coming to the aid of a lady," Tee had said and topped off her glass with more pinot noir. A middle-aged man at the table to her right lighted a cigarette and Tee waved away his smoke as she sipped her wine. "A woman should feel secure enough to show her gratitude," she said. Walter Rayno's new bride had applauded as the young Englishman ordered the photographer to leave the gallery. Tee had also looked at her husband, given a quick smile, and kissed the Englishman on his cheek. Walter Rayno tried to look very amused at the situation but he was not amused at all.

SUNLIGHT IS NOW a weak dull orange and angled though the four ceiling to floor windows in the living room. Walter Rayno has just rubbed more sodium hypochlorite onto the German's arms, the legs, his thick freckled belly. The German's skin is bleached white but there are raw patches where the chemical burned him. Blisters splotch his neck and the inner sides of his pale legs. The sodium hypochlorite has inflamed an already puffy face. His eyes have dried out and the edges of the eyes are crusted and yellow from the halogen lamp. This is the very least of it. The entire apartment on the Rue de Verneuil has the stink of new excrement. Walter Rayno's throat and nostrils are raw. He tries to smile and explain his work to the camera but how can anyone do a decent presentation when every breath is an effort?

THE DETECTIVE SERVICE in Paris emailed Walter Rayno last month to tell him they had found the German photographer.

This was right after Tee had sent her husband the documents to sign that would complete their divorce. Tee did not want any of his trust fund. She wanted no money at all, really. Her final letter to Walter Rayno had used the word 'freedom' nineteen times. The detective service said the German was a gentleman of habits. A person who was very easy to find, they had told him. Every weekend he would take a train into Paris. The gentleman ate at the same restaurants. He visited the same museums and parks. The gentleman was a widower with no children and no family and many cats. His wife had died of breast cancer six years ago. The gentleman painted some and sculpted some. He copied the masters and sold this art at his book shop in the Mitte district of Berlin.

People do what they have to do, Walter Rayno thinks. He must feed the old German by hand. Walter Rayno is the one who cleans up the piss and shit and scrubs the plastic sheet under the Louis XIV chair. He keeps the German's mouth taped or the man will scream and plead and curse him. The whimpering is unbearable. His whimpering goes on day and night. Sleep has become an infrequent thing. When allowed to speak, the German says the same words over and over. The words are not said in English. Other languages embarrass the old German.

"People do what they have to do," Walter Rayno says. "I am no different. I will do whatever is necessary," he tells the camera.

The German photographer turns his face toward Walter

Rayno's voice. *"Meine katzen haben keine Nahrung,"* the man says.

WALTER RAYNO HAD sat across from his bride at the neighborhood bistro, *Vins et Terroirs,* on Rue Saint Andre des Arts close to the Latin Quarter. He was eating his salmon salad and drinking chardonnay. The wine was crisp and icy on his tongue and on the back of his throat. It stopped the tension along his shoulders and forehead. He watched Tee poking a fork at her beef stew. Her face was in the shadows. Light from the bar reflected off the lenses of her tortoise shell glasses. Walter Rayno would forgive his new bride her petulance, her indiscretion. Who cared if she kissed a stranger on the cheek. The Englishman had chased away the German photographer simply to impress her. Walter Rayno believed men needed patience with women. Walter Rayno also believed he was more fair-minded than most young men his age. What was love, he thought, if not a man enduring the troubled and conflicted soul of the woman he loved?

Tee poured the last of the pinot noir from her carafe.

"I don't know if our marriage will work," Tee said. Her voice had a quiver to it. She was not looking at him. "I think you're a coward, Walter. I never knew that about you. I don't know if I can live with a coward."

Walter Rayno chewed a small forkful of his salmon salad. He took another slip of the cold chardonnay, a slice of baguette with whipped sweet butter.

"We're both tired," he said and blotted his mouth with a napkin. "The world will be a very different place tomorrow, believe me. Try the baguette," he told her. These people bake all day." His forefinger nudged the straw bread basket toward his bride. Men should never get caught up in a woman's drama, he thought. Men become lost in drama. At first Tee had been intrigued by him. That was the word she had used. Intrigued. Women usually left him feeling invisible and empty. Women did not get Walter Rayno. They did not understand him. They could not fathom the particulars of his mind, his talents and humor, his genius, his loyalty, especially his loyalty. Before Walter Rayno met Tee, women had not been worth his time.

"Norm let him off easy," Tee said. She smeared butter onto a slice of the warm baguette.

Norm was the name of the young Englishman who had chased the photographer from the Van Goghs. He had given Tee his business card after she kissed his cheek. Walter Rayno was not close enough to hear their conversation but he watched them. The young man had stepped too close to her. Tee seemed shy and could look at the Englishman for only a second or two.

Tee took a slip of the pinot noir to wash down the baguette.

"You can bleach the life out of these old paintings," Tee said to Walter. "The average person doesn't know how destructive a flash can be. They're totally oblivious, or they don't care. I mean a thousand flashes a day can wreak havoc on an old painting. Imagine the world without the *Starry Night* or the *Mona Lisa* or Monet's pictures of Venice." Tee leaned her elbows on the table. The lenses of her tortoise shell glasses reflected the light. "People should feel that sort of damage," she said. "Imagine being hurt like that, Walter."

"*Meine Katzen haben keine Nahrung*," the German photographer says.

The German is naked and sobbing but his eyes are dried from the halogen lamp and he cannot make tears.

The man now says the words in English.

"My cats have no food," he says.

Walter Rayno is standing behind the German in the same gray gabardine suit and matching silk tie. His hands are flat against the old man's cheeks and directing the face toward the video camera.

"Yesterday you told me you could not see," Walter Rayno says. "Tell this to the camera. "Describe how the halogen light has blinded you."

The German photographer tries raising his head toward the voice. Walter Rayno's hands grip the man's face and keep him aimed at the camera.

"*Meine Katzen hängen von mir ab*," the German says. His body is bloated, the flesh a slick white. Inflamed patches have blistered his knees, neck and the insides of his big thighs from the sodium hypochlorite. "My cats depend on me," the German says.

Evening has darkened Walter Rayno's apartment. The four ceiling to floor windows are opened onto the Rue de Verneuil and what is left of the daylight brings a pink color to the living room. Walter Rayno is using a 150 ampere Molarc to augment this light. It's too early for dinner but the restaurants below his apartment are cooking beef and fish and baking bread. The aroma reminds him of his dinner with Tee at the *Vins et Terroirs* on Rue Saint Andre des Arts near the Latin Quarter.

"What will happen to my cats?" the German photographer says. His voice is no more than a breath. Walter Rayno still has the German's face between his hands and aimed at the camera. He feels the old man's sweat under his fingers. Then the German says, "My cats worry me. Do your loved ones ever give you worry?"

Shadows are on the other side of the video camera and the Molarc light. Noise from the street enters through the open living room windows.

Walter Rayno is asking the German to describe the feeling of being blinded by the Halogen lamp but Walter Rayno isn't really interested. His thoughts are about Tee.

"I cannot believe that asshole is flashing a Van Gogh," his wife had said. "Can you believe that shit? Go talk to him," she'd said. "Tell him he might as well leave the goddamn picture in Sahara desert and let the sun fry it. Okay? Tell him that."

Walter Rayno's shoulders have started to tremble. The back of his throat burns from the stench of new excrement on the clear plastic sheet beneath the Louis XIV chair. Walter tries to imagine Tee watching his film. Her surprise, her satisfaction, her gratitude. Tee is teaching art history now in a small private school in London. Walter Rayno imagines Tee and her husband sitting on the sofa and watching the film together. Tee would be dressed in her sandals, her ivory blouse and short pleated skirt. Tee's husband is wearing his skinny black suit. Women usually leave Walter Rayno feeling invisible and empty. Women do not understand the particulars of Walter Rayno's mind, his talents and humor, his loyalty. Before Walter met Tee, women had not been worth his time.

American Daredevil

"If you're breathing, you're a daredevil."
—Noah Laws after his first public jump
Richmond, Virginia Fair Grounds
May 3rd, 1973

My father was taken to Norfolk General after a motorcycle accident, his first of many accidents, and I stayed with his brother who did not like the way my father lived his life. This was August, 1973, the year Scorsese directed Mean Streets, the year Grand Funk sang "We're an American Band." Except for mother, our family lived in Norfolk, Virginia, then. Uncle Nathan owned a white bungalow on Fayton Avenue off of Granby. The street had tall oaks along the curb and the roots were thick enough to crack the sidewalk. Leaves and dark branches stopped the sun and brought shade to everything. The smell of boxwood, roses and honeysuckle clung to the warm air. Living with Uncle Nathan meant lectures on how I ought to live my life and grievances against his older brother that started when they were boys and had not ended. My father's brother was a fussy man who needed his life just so. He also had never married and that was probably good for the species.

IN THOSE DAYS the best bike for jumping was a Harley XR-750. The daredevil Evel Knievel used the XR-750 in 1971 when he jumped 19 cars in Ontario, California. My father always said Evel had inspired him to become a great daredevil. After the Ontario jump father bought an XR-750. About a year later he quit the furniture and bedding store he owned with brother Nathan. This was when father asked my mother to get out the sewing machine and help him with his daredevil costume. My father had drawn a front, side and back view of the costume with a pencil on a yellow legal tablet. Arrows pointed to the cape and the high collar and the bell bottom pants. Next to the tail of each arrow he had printed the color he wanted, red for his cape, white for the high collar and shirt, a bright blue for the bell bottoms. He also said mother should outline his cape in white stars.

Father's real name is Noah Laws but you probably know him as The Immortal Law. He liked to say how his inspiration, Robert Knievel of Butte, Montana, knew enough to change his name to "Evel," and how this fine American had a certain flare, a genuine showmanship. That was also true of The Immortal Law. So much was Robert Knievel an inspiration that my father reinvented himself.

Mother said she knew my father would become a daredevil when he told her that the only fear he had was boredom.

"It took him twenty-two years but he did it." Mother said that to me in June of 1972 while she was standing by our open front door with a suitcase in each veined and bony hand. The breeze coming into the foyer was humid and carried her perfume, a scent of talc and watermelon. A hot morning sun hovered behind my mother and highlighted her curled hair. She looked small and skinny and dark. Then she said, "Don't look at me like that, Bryan. You're a young man now. And you're never home anyway. If your father and I see you twice a week we feel blessed."

"Didn't you say people should work on their problems?"

"I'm going back to North Carolina for awhile and live with my sister," she said. "I want to leave before the man kills himself."

My mother, Gloria Laws, *nee* Payton, had been a clinical psychologist for many years in downtown Norfolk and felt she knew a suicidal person when she saw one. Before attending graduate school at Virginia Commonwealth University and becoming a psychologist, mother had a good business making silver and turquoise rings and bracelets and selling her jewelry over the internet.

"He's *not* suicidal," I said. "You're just nervous."

"Is that what you think?" She sounded hurt, close to pouty.

Mother and I were standing in the white and black marble foyer and the sunlight glared through the open door and the bevelled glass that circled the doorframe. Sunlight reflected on the marble and the slick lacquered walls.

I supported your father in a lot of things," she said. "But crazy isn't one of them."

> "You want to be a daredevil and laugh in death's face? Fine."
> —my father and Uncle Nathan on the showroom floor of Laws' Furnishings and Bedding, 1971

"I have rules in my house, Bryan. One *main* rule has to do with shoes on a bed." Uncle Nathan stood in the doorway of the little guest room that he had assigned to me. He removed a plastic beige inhaler from the pocket of his chinos and took a hit. My father's brother had asthma and he'd had asthma throughout his life. Nathan slept in the bedroom next to mine and at night I could hear him forcing each breath, long phlegmy gasps. The house had a heavy lavender disinfectant smell. I think Uncle Nathan envied my father in many ways and one of these ways was my father's good health. "In my house we will respect the property of others," Nathan said. "In my house we keep our shoes on the floor."

I was sitting on the bed watching *The Flip Wilson Show* on a small TV. At home I never put my shoes on the bed but I do not think people remember everyday courtesies when nothing around them is familiar. My stomach felt tight and I could imagine myself on the street with no home and no place to feel safe. I had turned on the TV to find a face I felt comfortable with and liked.

From the day Noah Laws bought his XR-750 I started believing my father and my uncle had nothing in common but their parents and their recliners. This was just a fact as far as I was concerned. I am very much like my father. In those days Noah Laws was tall and slender and had black hair combed straight back. This is me today. I am my father's son and I do not mind confessing it. After Noah Laws bought his Harley XR-750 he started to dress with a little style. My father would wear blue pin-striped suits to synagogue and his shirts were white and starched and had stiff perfect collars. Uncle Nathan also had black hair but he was short and looked like a troll with tiny ears.

"Maybe your father's place is a barn but not here," my uncle said.

Our house was three times bigger than Nathan's two bedroom bungalow. Father worked the stocks and had what my mother called "family investments." Uncle Nathan did not like him for that either.

The guest room had red, white and green flowered wallpaper and a maple wood bed, nightstand and bureau that had a ranch look. These pieces were always fifty percent off at Laws' Furnishings and Beddings. A dark stain was on the ceiling in the far corner of the room next to the open window. A metal bucket was beneath the stain and every now and again a single drop of water would leave the ceiling and hit the bucket with a tinny plop.

I WAS SIXTEEN when mother ran for her life, but I thought having a suicidal father called The Immortal Law was much better than having a regular father who owned a cheap furniture and bedding store with his brother. More, really. The Immortal Law gave me courage I did not think I had, courage I suspected my regular father lacked.

I could not imagine brave acts coming from a man who sold furnishings and bedding. A boy cannot become courageous if there is no one to teach him how to do it. The man had a wife who complained about him. The man ate Quaker Oats and wheat toast for breakfast. The man wore Bermuda shorts and wing tips on summer weekends. My father began work at eight-fifteen in the morning and did not get home until nine-thirty or ten o'clock at night. He wanted only peace and quiet but would also ask me questions I could not answer.

"What's with you and sports?" he'd say during a TV commercial.

"I don't want to break something."

"Kids play sports," he'd say.

"You can lose an eye." I did not understand the reason for sports.

"We're talking baseball here," he told me.

Sports scared me. Other things scared me, heights, for instance, public speaking, girls who liked me, gym locker rooms, bigger boys who tortured kids scared me, what hid under my bed at night, teachers who would ask me questions in class, anyone I did not know, camping in the woods, choking on anything scared me, what hid under the ocean, adults who looked at me funny, any type of weapon, any food my mother did not cook, door to door salesmen scared me. I had a list. But "heights" was the leader in my fear parade. I used to watch TV programs where fathers taught their sons to box and to go beat up the neighborhood bullies. My father wanted to watch the evening news in his old recliner while eating snacks from a bowl on a blond wood TV tray. He worked hard but did not like his job and did not like his brother or the demanding customers who wanted sofas and chairs in colors the store did not have and the company did not make and would not make if the company was set on fire.

Then Noah Laws bought his Harley XR-750, and my mother and I did not know what to think or do, especially me. Bad boys rode Harleys, the Hell's Angels, the Pagans, the War-locks, the Breed, the Wheels of Soul, the Ghetto Riders, guys with facial hair and bandanas and tattoos. They had tattoos of roses dripping blood, tattoos of snakes that wrapped about a bicep. They had attitudes you did not want to fuck with.

"YOUR FATHER HAS a death wish," mother had said. She said it that day in the foyer with the front door open and the sun-light reflecting on everything. The suitcases she held in each hand were a tan and green plaid and had large silver catches. The weight of these suitcases seemed to stretch her skimpy pale arms.

"But you sewed his costume."

"What can I say?" she said and shrugged. "I thought it was a phase."

"Thinking is what you do *before* your daredevil work. Once you're out there, you leave thinking alone."
—The Immortal Law on Sport's World TV
May, 1973

WATER DROPS APPEARED on the dark stain in the far corner of ceiling and the drops fell into the metal bucket beneath near the bedroom window. The drops hit the water in the bucket but the sounds had no rhythm.

"Your father brought this on himself," Uncle Nathan said to me. He took the beige plastic inhaler from the pocket of his pressed chinos. My uncle had these inhalers in every room of his house. When he was annoyed his breathing got erratic. He closed his thin lips about the plastic inhaler and breathed the mist. "What can I say?" Uncle Nathan said. "The man doesn't know how to take others into consideration. That's always been his problem, if you ask me."

Uncle Nathan was a safe man who thought my father was a crazy man. My uncle was a head and a half shorter than my father and he had a thick neck and shoulders and liked wearing open collar beige and white shirts that showed coiled chest hair. His brown pleated pants draped a pair of scuffed wing-tips. Nathan was health conscious and had a morning and night vitamin regime that started with a nutrient dense multivitamin with minerals, an additional 1,000 mgs of time released vitamin C, 1,200 mgs of Omega-3/Omega-6 Salmon oil, 1,200 mgs calcium with vitamin D, 30 mgs of coenzyme Q-10, 640 mgs X2 of flush-free Niacin, Glucosamine Sulfate for the joints, and an 81mg aspirin. He also smoked three low tar and nicotine cigarettes a day, one after each meal for digestive purposes.

"The first born is always a crazy child," Uncle Nathan said and patted the sweat from his neck with a white cotton hand-kerchief. "Very spoiled and crazy, let me tell you," my uncle said. "When we were boys your father always had to have it his way. Not that I begrudge him. And in your grandmother's eyes, God rest her soul, your father could do no wrong. He was an angel on earth." Uncle Nathan took another hit off his plastic inhaler. "What does your father know from motorcycles?" he said and wheezed out a tiny breath. "He's a crazy man who can't change a tire."

I was watching the last fifteen minutes of *The Flip Wilson Show* on the portable TV I had set up at the foot of my bed. A night breeze came through the open window and there was the smell of neighborhood dinners that had been cooked earlier, mainly fish and beef. These odors were filtered through Uncle Nathan's lavender disinfectant. Water from the dark stain in the ceiling continued to plop into the metal bucket at the corner of the room by the window.

"My father isn't crazy," I said.

"Relax, sonny boy. When you're older you'll see."

I wanted to tell Uncle Nathan that *he* was the crazy person, not my father, that people in glass houses shouldn't throw stones. According to mother, Nathan was a big germiphobe. "He sprays his house with enough disinfectant to do heart surgery in the room of his choice," mother would say. "God forbid you had a cold or the flu and needed him to do an errand. He'd refused to answer a phone." This was absolutely true. Nathan also washed his hands raw if you looked at him funny. Uncle Nate was not a person fit to discuss sanity issues.

My father did not quit the furnishings and bedding business right away. He was forty years old then and I could not recall anything impulsive about him. This man looked before he leaped. This man practiced his daredevil stunts in a weedy vacant lot behind our house every day after work and on weekends. My father rented a bulldozer and personally shaped a red dirt track in a figure eight. The track crossed grass and clay mounds and into freshly dug gullies. Noah Laws practiced for close to a year, maybe longer, and the weather did not matter to him. He was the mailman of daredevils, neither rain nor snow nor gloom of night stopped my father and his Harley from their task.

He built plywood ramps that ended where a long stacked pile of empty oil drums began. There were enormous wrought iron hoops wrapped in cloth that my father soaked in gas and set on fire. Sometimes I would watch him with binoculars from our back kitchen window. Sometimes I would go into my bedroom and shut the door and lie on my bed and listen to the revving of his motorcycle engine. My mother had left us to live in North Carolina. I did not need my father to die.

Noah Laws slid across the wet clay track in a chilled October rain. He tumbled over the front wheel to meet the ice of December. This man on a mission, this new daredevil. He had found his purpose, that indefinable nuance that can turn a black and white life into color. No longer did my father slump into his velour recliner each evening and hide behind *The Norfolk Ledger* and TV comedies. His cheeks had a flush and his eyes were bright and alive.

My father even smelled different. Laws' Furnishings and Bedding had a cardboard and plastic smell from the packing crates. Adding to this was Nathan spraying the storage and show rooms with his lavender scented disinfectant. That was my father's smell until the afternoon he bought his Harley XR-750 and began practicing on the figure eight track in the vacant lot behind our house for his new career as a daredevil. Then Noah Laws smelled of mud and gasoline. He smelled like somebody having a good time.

"Let's go play catch," my father said to me one evening. He had leaped from his velour recliner and clapped his hands, his thin long fingers with their uneven nails. "I bought us these gloves and a couple of balls. Gamache Sports was having a fifty percent off sale. What do you say, honey?"

I was sixteen years old and the man called me "honey."

"My name Bryan," I said.

"I know your name. You're my son."

"I'm just saying," I said.

My father was pressing one of the new white baseballs into his glove and he stopped to glance up at me. The smile on his narrow face had drained off, his lips parted but without expression, his brow pinched into a concerned look.

"When did you become such an old man?" he said.

A week later my father tried jumping twelve ice cream trucks at the Virginia Beach Amphitheater and his rear tire hit the edge of the last truck. That mistake threw him from his Harley XR-750 and he broke his left wrist, left knee, six ribs and fractured his hip. He stayed unconscious in Norfolk General for twenty-two days.

> "Evel Knievel broke 433 of his own bones. That got him into the Guinness Book of World Records. But that's a record I'm willing to let Evel keep."
> —A Norfolk Ledger interview with
> The Immortal Law at Norfolk General, 1973

THE DAY BEFORE the hospital called to say my father was again in this world and talking to the staff, Uncle Nathan had climbed to the tar and asphalt roof of his house to repair the shingle that had caused the water problem on the ceiling of the guest room. Afternoon clouds from the Chesapeake had come in behind a sunny morning and the sky looked ready for a storm. The breeze was warm and gusty and smelled of boxwood and honeysuckle. I was next to the ladder watching Nathan with a hand cupped over my brow. A silvery glare seeped from the clouds. He was lying stomach down on the peak of the roof, his short legs hugging the two slanting sides for balance. Four bright metal nails were pressed between his lips. He would drive one nail into a new asphalt shingle and reach to his mouth for another nail. I remember being very impressed with that, the precision of it, the bravery, not only had Uncle Nathan climbed onto a roof but he was doing an activity.

"Are you okay?" I shouted this to him.

"Why shouldn't I be okay?" He shouted back and hit another nail into the dark asphalt roof. Then he said, "You think your big shot daredevil father is better than me? You think I can't fix a roof?"

The sky was a deeper gray than an hour ago, the clouds thicker, and the breeze rushed through the oak trees and turned the leaves on their faded backs and revealed the twist and the knots of black branches. Rain was ten or fifteen minutes away from us and it draped down from the sky and flapped like a stiff cloth. I felt the warm air go damp and the smell of the boxwood and the honeysuckle had become stronger.

"Come down here," I said but he did not hear me and I circled my mouth with my hands and again shouted at him to come down, to finish the roof tomorrow, or a week from tomorrow. Who cared, really? I did not need him in the hospital, too. "What's wrong with you?" I said, yelled it.

Uncle Nathan's hair whipped about his face. The bright metal nail he had been holding fell between his fingers and skidded down the dark roof and onto the grass beside me. He reached into the front pocket of his shirt and retrieved the beige plastic inhaler. I was next to the ladder and I could see panic bleeding up into his face. His hand had a tremor and the inhaler slipped from his fingers as the plastic lip was about to reach his mouth. The inhaler followed the path of the nail down the slanted roof.

I remembered Uncle Nathan's face as I climbed the ladder with his plastic inhaler in my right hand, climbed the ladder without a thought or fear in my head. I'd concentrate on Nathan, his desperation, the anxious pleading look. When he finally grasped his fingers about the inhaler and breathed in the mist, the color and the calm began showing in his face.

"There are things I think about before I do them," my father would say. "Then there are things I do and think about them later." Noah Laws taught me that, the furnishings and bedding salesman from Norfolk, Virginia, the big deal daredevil.

My father did not return to Laws' Furnishings and Bedding, and over the next two years Noah and Gloria Laws divorced. My father toured the East Coast and the Midwest for close to fifteen years. He was seldom away from me and his home for more than a day or two, playing mostly fair grounds and sporting events. I was older then, and getting myself ready for college. There were many cheering crowds for my father, many, many crowds. And I knew he thought he had a better life. The Immortal Law also had many accidents, let me tell you, but he always stayed a hundred bones shy of Evel Knievel.

Fomite

A fomite is a medium capable of transmitting infectious organisms from one individual to another.

"The activity of art is based on the capacity of people to be infected by the feelings of others." Tolstoy, *What Is Art?*

Writing a review on Amazon, Good Reads, Shelfari, Library Thing or other social media sites for readers will help the progress of independent publishing. To submit a review, go to the book page on any of the sites and follow the links for reviews. Books from independent presses rely on reader to reader communications.

For more information or to order any of our books, visit
http://www.fomitepress.com/FOMITE/Our_Books.html

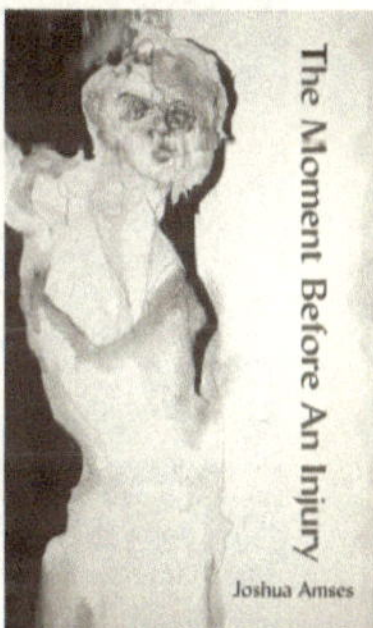

*The Moment
Before an Injury*
Joshua Amses

*Nothing Beside
Remains*
Jaysinh Birjépatil

*The Way None
of This Happened*
Mike Breiner

Victor Rand
David Brizer

*Summer on the
Cold War Planet*
Paula Closson Buck

*Cycling in Plato's
Cave*
David Cavanagh

Fomite

Where There Are Two or More
Elizabeth Genovise

The Hundred Yard Dash Man
Barry Goldensohn

When You Remember Deir Yassin
R. L. Green

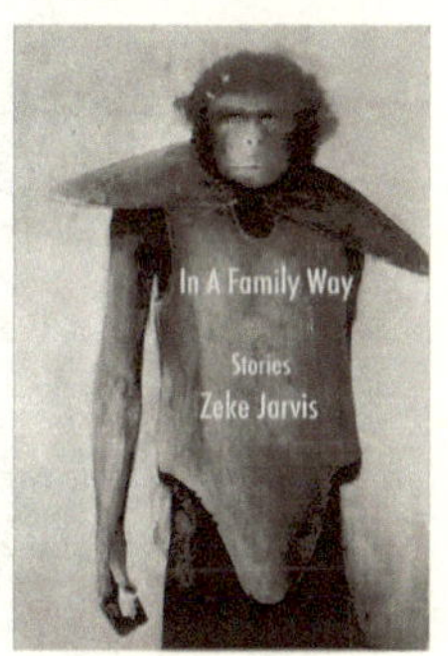

In A Family Way
Zeke Jarvis

A Free, Unsullied Land
Maggie Kast

Feminist on Fire
Coleen Kearon

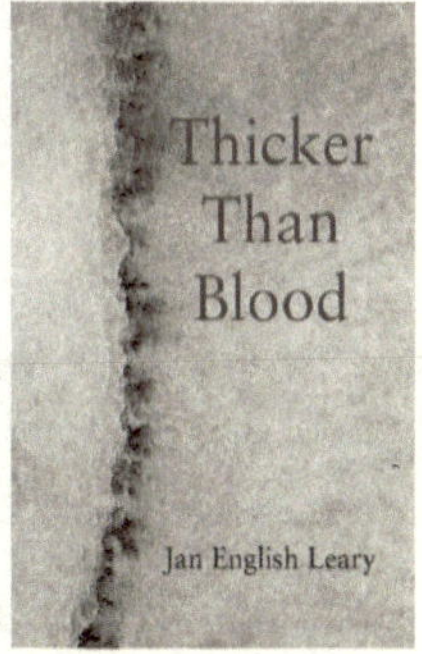

Thicker Than Blood
Jan English Leary

A Guide to the Western Slope
Roger Lebovitz

Confessions of a Carnivore
Diane Lefer

Fomite

Unborn Children of America
Michele Markarian

Museum of the Americas
Gary Lee Miller

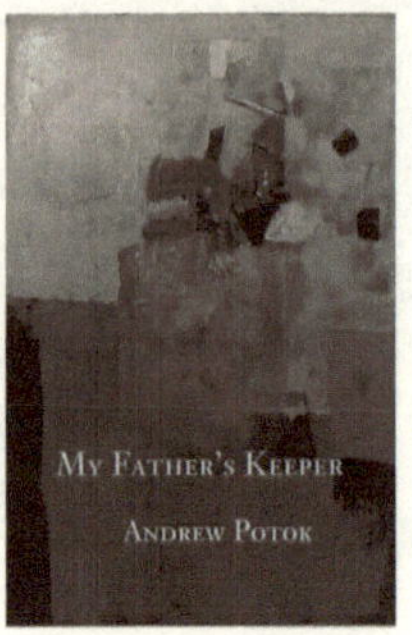

My Father's Keeper
Andrew Potok

The Hole That Runs Through Utopia
Joseph D. Reich

Companion Plants
Kathryn Roberts

Rafi's World
Fred Russell

My Murder and Other Local News
David Schein

Planet Kasper Volume Two
Peter Schumann

Bread & Sentences
Peter Schumann

Fomite

Industrial Oz
Scott T. Starbuck

Principles of Navigation
Lynn Sloan

Among Angelic Orders
Susan Thoma

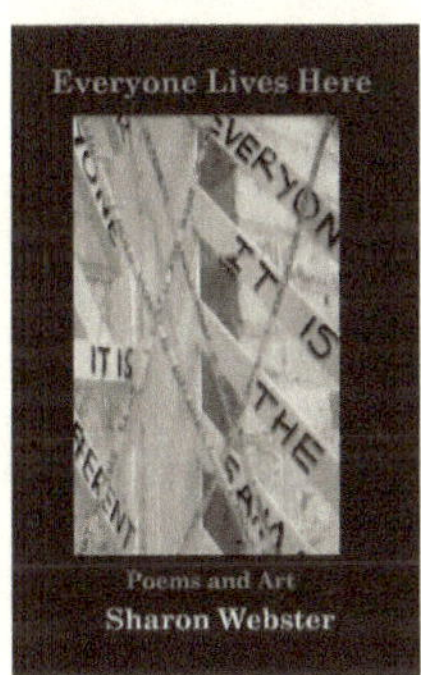

Everyone Lives Here
Sharon Webster

The Falkland Quartet
Tony Whedon

*The Return of
Jason Green*
Suzi Wizowaty

*The Inconveniece
of the Wings*
Silas Dent Zobal

Fomite

More Titles from Fomite...

Joshua Amses — *Raven or Crow*

Joshua Amses — *The Moment Before an Injury*

Jaysinh Birjepatil — *The Good Muslim of Jackson Heights*

Antonello Borra — *Alfabestiario*

Antonello Borra — *AlphaBetaBestiario*

Jay Boyer — *Flight*

Dan Chodorkoff — *Loisada*

Michael Cocchiarale — *Still Time*

Greg Delanty — *Loosestrife*

Zdravka Evtimova — *Carts and Other Stories*

Anna Faktorovich — *Improvisational Arguments*

Derek Furr — *Suite for Three Voices*

Stephen Goldberg — *Screwed*

Barry Goldensohn — *The Listener Aspires to the Condition of Music*

Greg Guma — *Dons of Time*

Andrei Guruianu — *Body of Work*

Ron Jacobs — *The Co-Conspirator's Tale*

Ron Jacobs — *Short Order Frame Up*

Ron Jacobs — *All the Sinners Saints*

Kate MaGill — *Roadworthy Creature, Roadworthy Craft*

Ilan Mochari — *Zinsky the Obscure*

Fomite

Jennifer Moses — *Visiting Hours*

Sherry Olson — *Four-Way Stop*

Janice Miller Potter — *Meanwell*

Jack Pulaski — *Love's Labours*

Charles Rafferty — *Saturday Night at Magellan's*

Joseph D. Reich — *The Derivation of Cowboys & Indians*

Joseph D. Reich — *The Housing Market*

Fred Russell — *Rafi's World*

Peter Schumann — *Planet Kasper, Volume 1*

L. E. Smith — *The Consequence of Gesture*

L. E. Smith — *Travers' Inferno*

L. E. Smith — *Views Cost Extra*

Susan Thomas — *The Empty Notebook Interrogates Itself*

Tom Walker — *Signed Confessions*

Susan V. Weiss — *My God, What Have We Done?*

Peter Mathiessen Wheelwright — *As It Is On Earth*